SACCHARIN CYANIDE
short stories

Anna Livia

Published by Onlywomen Press, Ltd.
Radical Feminist and Lesbian publishers,
38 Mount Pleasant, London WC1X 0AP

Printed and bound in Denmark by Norhaven.
Typeset by Columns, Reading, Berks, UK.

Cover painting © Gina Gilmore.

"Angel Alice" was first published in the anthology, THE PIED
PIPER: lesbian feminist fiction, ed. A. Livia and L. Mohin,
Onlywomen Press, London, 1989. "Spaceship to the Good Planet"
was first published in the journal, Sinister Wisdom, No. 37,
U.S.A., 1989. "Car Spray" was first published in the journal,
Lesbian Ethics, Vol. 3, no. 3, U.S.A., 1989. "Saccharin Cyanide"
will be published in the anthology, IN AND OUT OF TIME: lesbian
feminist fiction, ed. Patricia Duncker, Onlywomen Press, London,
1990. "The Promised Land Recedes into a Grey Horizon" will be
published in the anthology, FINDING THE LESBIANS, ed. Julia
Penelope, Crossing Press, U.S.A., 1990. "Lust, and the Other
Half" will be published in the anthology, BODY AND SOUL, ed.
Judith Barrington, Eighth Mountain Press, U.S.A., 1990.

British Library Cataloguing in Publication Data
Livia, Anna, 1955–
    Saccharin cyanide
    I. Title
    823'.914 [F]

ISBN 0–906500–35–4

for Bertha Harris

CONTENTS

DIFFERENTLY MOTIVATED

Rennen received with equanimity the summons to Tet's office for an informal chat. The exam results had just gone up; it would not be unusual for her tutor to wish to discuss them with her. Anything else should come as a complete surprise: surprise would be her greatest protection, greatest proof of innocence. She had passed. An ungraded pass, no credits, no honours. Without seeing the examiners' comments, she assumed 98% in Linguistics, 94% in Gden, Xta'mba, Sing, Pitjant and Fortrain – the languages of the five planets, known collectively as Sipifo; 60% in Teaching Practice; 40% in Theory of Education; 25% in Pure and Applied Pedagogy.

"Rennen," said Tutor Tet once his student was seated and attentive, "I have your exam results. A mediocre 59%. I would like you to explain."

"A bit disappointing," Rennen felt safe to admit, "But at least I passed."

"Don't take that tone with me, young lady," said Tutor Tet, "You're not some plodder who should be happy to scrape through and grateful thanks. Your marks on individual papers span 99% to 23%."

"I would have done alright if Pedagogy and Theory of Ed weren't weighted to count twice," said Rennen as sulkily as she could manage.

"You were sitting for a Postgraduate Licence in Education," snarled Tutor Tet, it irked him to state the obvious. He wished to talk with Rennen equal to equal and he rarely found, or admitted, a woman as his equal. "You scored barely 33% on the Education side. This will not do."

"But clearly it will," Rennen was obliged to observe, "Because I have an overall pass."

"Why do you settle for so little? What are you playing at? You made no effort whatever on your Education papers and precious little on T.P. from what I've been told. Fear of success? Afraid to really apply yourself? If you do no work at all and still pass you can go on believing that if only you did try you'd do brilliantly?"

"Perhaps that's it," Rennen agreed.

"Or might you be Differently Motivated?" Tutor Tet rattled on. "Differently Motivated" was the new euphemism for lazy. Since it was no longer economically necessary for all able-bodied adults to work, a certain amount of alternative motivation was permitted. Young people might, for example, take two years off to practice Applied Onanism and many artists, before they became galactic sellers and so, productive, could register and apply to the Office of Utter Penury for subsistence without term. Most people still preferred to work: the money was incomparable and they liked being responsible cogs.

"Are you planning to apply for artistic classification?" Tutor Tet pursued.

"Oh no," replied Rennen with easy surprise. "My Psych tests show no hint of different motivation."

"No," Tutor Tet concurred. "You score your 70% average every time we test you. Any higher, we'd be on the look out for fanaticism. Much lower, and we'd haul you in for an aptitude scan."

"I think I score average on motivation because I genuinely am pretty average," said Rennen with resignation.

"We call you in each time one of your tutors expresses alarm, about once a month, and you score

70%," sighed Tutor Tet. "We insert trick questions to make sure you're not responding by rote, having such wide experience of our tests," here he laughed a little, "And you politely jump them, time restrictions not permitting you to reply fully to all questions."

The question in Rennen's mind was: what was Tutor Tet's motivation? Until she divined that, she was obliged to play out this lengthy stalemate. Tutor Tet must be tiring of the game too.

"I played the video of your admission interview, Rennen," he said, "You were brilliant. Quite wonderful. We all thought so. Then I played the tape back, watched and listened again to see how you did it, what it was that was so impressive."

Rennen waited.

"You answered our questions in swift shorthand, then moved the conversation on to your strong point. Even those of us who noticed that your answers were cursory at best were too excited by your speciality to pull you up. Perfect interview technique. Of course our questions bored us as much as the standard, required answers; of course we preferred to be fascinated by you. Once established on the course, you simply relied on your extraordinary skill to raise your overall totals, sat back and did nothing for the rest of the year."

Rennen smiled apologetically. Nothing illegal about any of that; all quite normal.

"What I want to know," demanded Tutor Tet, drawing his face abruptly close to hers, "is why?"

Rennen shrugged with a self-deprecating laugh.

"Don't bother," Tutor Tet burst out, "Can't you see your position is perilous?"

Rennen could not see that it was. All this sounded very much like the standard tutor outburst she had had to endure over her years in higher, tertiary, further and advanced education.

"I thought I might make a good teacher," said Rennen simply, "I listen to what people say."

"Oh bullshit, cowshit, horse manure," shouted her Tutor, "You have absolutely no intention of teaching. Or of performing any other productive task for which

3

you have qualified over the years. You must have more diplomas than the Director of the Institute."

This was true. She had.

"All mediocre," he added.

Also true. Perhaps he would come to the point soon. It was her right as Citizen of the Five Planets to follow any course for which she could gain entry by competitive exam and interview. She found she could gain entry to most.

"You listen to what people say!" blustered Tutor Tet, "Whatever part of the galaxy they come from, whatever organs they use for speech, you hear what they say, whether it's one of your languages or not. You know what they have rubbed, blown, vibrated, imploded, banged or trilled to produce the utterance and, what's more, you can write the whole thing out in the phonetic script of one's choosing and repeat it, sound for sound."

This too Rennen had heard before, though not usually hurled as such an accusation. Did her Tutor feel she had in some way deprived him of something?

"I understand the principles," Rennen began to explain courteously.

Tutor Tet interrupted her.

"Very often you don't understand the languages!"

"I could," Rennen admitted, "I could learn them, but I have Sipifo and I find I prefer principles to actual syntax and lexicon."

"You translate, perfectly, from languages you have never studied."

"Ah yes," said Rennen, "But I can't translate into them. Only from."

As long as they were discussing her language skills she was, relatively, safe. But the interview had gone on for quite long enough; he ought to let her go now he'd had his explosion.

"Rennen," he said more calmly, "Why did you decide to scrape through Theory of Education?"

Rennen sighed but said nothing.

"I checked your library loans. You borrowed all the set texts in the first two weeks of term, then you returned them and did not set foot in the library again.

4

What was it you read that turned you against
education?"
A new tack. It was becoming clear that Tutor Tet was
onto something. Rennen cast her mind over the
possibilities. If he'd checked her library loans, had he
also checked her credit ratings? Well, of course he
had. She always dealt in cash which was unusual, but
not very, so her credit would show poor to very poor
with little movement. Most planets paid cash for her
translations, transcriptions and transliterations, believing the stories they heard of the enormous tax
burdens on Gden, Rennen's home planet. When she
travelled offworld, she would divide the journey into
small units so cash settlements would cause no stir:
little hops from Gden to Moonbase to Sing and from
Sing to Xta'mba. But everyone slips up somewhere
and the best security measure is to prevent the
question being asked.

What now? she wondered. An ideological stand,
perhaps. Yes, best take one of those.

"I am proud to score 40% for Theory of Education.
One cent higher and I would be obliged to consider
myself the most loathsome abomination known to the
Five Planets."

At last he had got her going, thought Tutor Tet.

"The Theory of Education is a many volumed
handbook for the justification of oppression. Specifically: the oppression of the uninformed by the learned.
It is a lethal ideological tool for maintaining the status
quo. If we came across a manual for the justification of
slavery and an accompanying examination which gave
an automatic 'nil' to any answer implying that slavery
itself was wrong, we would disgust ourselves, would
we not, if we did anything but fail the exam. We
would hope to achieve a total of zero and count any
points scored as marks against us. If I had failed my
Theory of Education Exam, I would have failed the
whole course and be obliged to pay for my tuition, a
tithe not placed upon those who pass. I therefore
scored the mark of least disgrace compatible with
financial impunity."

Tutor Tet would have to respond to such a speech. His

career was on the line. He was an educationalist, for Gden's sake.

"Why did you apply for this course in the first place?" he asked, icily.

This was the real question.

"If you want to avoid the daily annoyance of work, why not register as an Artist and apply for Total Penury. You don't live much above subsistence as it is."

From which Rennen learned two useful facts: Tutor Tet had indeed checked her credit movement and, since he had now suggested it twice, he did believe that secretly she was Differently Motivated and buying time in order to pursue some creative hobby. All creativity was termed a hobby until, or unless, it made money. Tutor Tet was coming very close and the set of his shoulders assured Rennen he had no intention of giving up till he was satisfied. She would have to satisfy him.

"I will tell you what you want to know," she said, "But only if you sign a non-divulgence clause."

Tutor Tet, despite his intensive training, his increasing conviction that Rennen was the one, gasped. With all her years — near on two decades — in one top ranking academic institution after another, with access to high level information which, although not classified, could be very useful to a foreign power if put together in a certain way — he had no doubt it would be put together — her skill at breaking communications down into base parts, analysing and reconstructing them so that even coded messages could be relayed — the code cracked later — Rennen was the perfect spy. It only remained to discover which of the other Four Planets was employing her and, out of idle curiosity, how they were making it worth her while.

"Hippocratic non-divulgence?" he joked. Doctors signed a non-divulgence as soon as they qualified so their patients would feel free to disclose the intimate and disgusting nature of their ailments and how they might have contracted them. Lawyers, too, of course. And sexual partners. Was that what she was doing? Asking him to incriminate himself in advance by signing a document which, since he was neither a doctor nor a lawyer, and it could not be supposed that she knew of his special function as Planetary Agent, must mean he had engaged in sexual encounters with a student.

"I don't know," he said, as though considering the matter.

Rennen sat back and waited. He could still expose her. Different Motivation was not a criminal offence, though it was considered immature, unbalanced and even psychologically unsound. But her motivation was so different most planets would consider incarceration on some pretext, if not shrink-wrapping and aversion therapies. She supposed she might live through it; nothing short of death would make her respond to any other stimulus than the single strange call which was her present motivator. She might live, but as it was also possible she might not, she had better avoid the confrontation. Even if Tutor Tet signed a Non-divulgence, he could pass her story on as a learning parable where no accusation was made but sufficient traces had been left for the hearer to identify the guilty protagonist as Rennen. How many permanent students with perfect phonetic recall were there, for example.

Tutor Tet concluded that he might as well sign. Gden Security would understand the circumstances and, seeing the prize he would have brought in, overlook the irregularity. If Gden Educational decided to sack him for sexual harassment, it did not really matter: he would probably have to change cover anyway once he'd collared Rennen.

"I will sign," he said, pressed the relevant buttons on his console and an official form flipped out of the printer.

"Registering for courses gives me more money than I would get on Total Penury and affords me time to pursue my sole real interest. Artistic persons are subject to endless registration and output checks which I could not tolerate and which would hinder my vocation. On a course I simply opt for assessment

7

by examination instead of course-work and pass the final exam to avoid paying costs," Rennen explained. "I am, as you suggested, Differently Motivated."

"And what is your motivation?" Tutor Tet enquired, to cover his hand's movement on the console, testing the recording equipment.

There was no word for it. Rennen searched each language she'd come across, but none of the official versions accorded her Difference the significance of a denotative term. If she said she was "a woman's woman", an easily understood designation among the women's women of Mbarri, in accepted speech this would mean a gynecologist. Here on Gden she might say a "Sapphist" to women like herself, but everyone else would understand a poet who uses a particular, rather conservative, metre. "Lesbian" was, except in certain minority circumstances, a geographical description. An "invert" was, commonly, an interior decorator with a flair for greenery. "I sleep with women" implied that she had grown up in close quarters with many sisters.

"I am motivated by women," announced Rennen, unconsciously picking the Gden Security slang for a spy with a female spymaster. Tutor Tet nodded at this admission, steepled his fingers to mark the solemnity of the occasion, and said,

"Continue. I understand perfectly," adding so that she would see he really did understand, "It may even be something of a relief to you to speak at last."

"I had a particular woman in mind," Rennen sighed, "Luth Cievale, a student of advanced Ensk."

"Indeed," remarked Tutor Tet. Ensk was spoken on Ardesh which, far from being one of the Five Planets, was the other side of the Trade Barrier. The picture began to take shape. He made a note on his console to follow up this Luth Cievale later.

"I was mad, passionate, crazy in love with her. Couldn't think of anything else. She was already having an affair, one of long standing: ten years, and she wouldn't look at me. Oh you know how it is: sometimes she would, sometimes she wouldn't. Blow hot, blow cold. Drove me beetle-browed. Couldn't tell

8

if she was interested in me or putting on a display for her lover. I knew she was going back to Ardesh for three months language saturation and I reckoned that was my best chance. Her lover, woman called Tanzeki Mestrino, who's something in cromagnetons, would never be able to get offworld to visit her, so there poor Luth would be: no lover and much emptiness. Fair bet she wouldn't team up with a local for the duration; you know how strict Ardesh is about fraternisation with outworlders. They get sent to Outer Kazbek soon as look at you. I decided to register for a course with a foreign language element and follow Luth to Ardesh."

"But Ensk isn't one of your languages," objected Tutor Tet, wanting to get the story whole and complete.

"No," Rennen agreed, "But Ensk and Xta'mba are both Meno-dentane so they share the same roots. Oh, two thousand years ago but stimulating to research."

"Which, naturally, is what you said you were going to do," said Tutor Tet obligingly.

"Naturally," said Rennen. "There I was in the middle of Ardesh City, not speaking a word of Ensk, searching for Luth when all I had was the name of the institute where she was studying. Fortunately I could pronounce the name though, as I'm sure you know, the Ardashi have eight more points of articulation than we do and their ruminant diaphragm resonance is quite a poser to reproduce."

"I'm sure you did splendidly."

"I couldn't ask for directions because I wouldn't have understood them and city maps are not available to outworlders. I had no contacts for the black market. So, what I did: I took the trolleybus to Malinki Prospekt, the central boulevard of Ardesh City, assuming that such a prestigious institute would be situated near the main concourse."

"How could you tell it was prestigious?"

"It's called the 'Lerrinskaya Ensk Institut', I transliterate. Since Lerrinsky is the big hero, his institute has to be prestigious. So there I am, middle of Malinki Prospekt, not a clue whether to go left or right, up or down. Then I spotted an ice cream seller.

The Ardashi love ice cream. Stalls everywhere, fortunately for me. I went up to the nearest one, bought an ice cream – gesticulate and smile fashion – and said, enunciating clearly: 'Lerrinskaya Ensk Institut tak'. I gathered 'tak' meant 'thanks'; it seemed to go down well. The ice cream seller looked puzzled. Pleasant but puzzled. For a second I doubted my phonetic skills; then I realised: she couldn't hear above the noise of the trolleybuses. I wrote the name down in big careful letters. She nodded with enthusiastic comprehension, pointed back across the road and rattled off a series of directions which I assumed must have meant: 'Other side of the Prospekt, take the first left, second right, over a little bridge with stone lions holding the parapet in their mouths, along to the end of the walkway, through a small public garden and it's straight in front of you, you fall onto it, can't miss'. Only, of course, I didn't understand a word. I followed the direction of her gesticulating arm and crossed the road. There I repeated the operation with another ice cream seller. Again I had, respectfully, to ignore everything she said and simply continue in the first direction indicated. I consumed eight ice creams in this fashion but I reached the Lerrinskaya Ensk Institut without once getting lost or doubling back on my tracks.

"I stood in an imposing marble hallway holding out my piece of paper for all the world like Caspar Hauser. I had turned it over and written 'Luth Cievale' on the back. People issued out of doors on the upper gallery, descended the stairs and came to get a closer look at me and my paper. Others crowded out of downstairs classrooms, from along dark corridors, or peered in at the window. 'Luth Cievale' they said aloud, 'Luth Cievale'. The name was passed up and down the crowd like a small child or a bunch of fresh flowers on a packed trolleybus. It surged up the stairs and swept along the upper gallery, flowing into the open classrooms. The Institute was soon filled with the sound of her name. Some believed that Luth was me; others that I was calling for my Tutor. By now I

10

believe there is a secret cult who hail 'Luth' as the name of the Messiah.

"Eventually different people began to try out different languages. Some but a few words, others long complicated, formal paragraphs of enquiry, welcome and the assurance of their devoted respect. Someone hit on Pitjant and I explained my business. I was told that Nalya would come and take my hand. This was indeed the truth for soon a young woman appeared, smiled encouragingly and said: 'I am Nalya. I will take your hand'. She led me along corridors, up and down stairs, into and through offices, addressed remarks to other persons phrased in what I had begun to recognise as the interrogative and always including the two words 'Luth Cievale'. Finally, and still holding my hand, she looked triumphant and announced: 'I have found Luth'.

"We left the Institute by a side exit, majestic with lions and lilies. In the garden Nalya stopped and said, 'I cannot leave but presently a boy will come and he will take your hand.' This also proved to be true. As my left hand was dropped on one side, my right hand was picked up on the other and I was guided out through black iron railings, along a new series of streets and round corners until I was placed before a bell with a number of words in the Ensk alphabet and including the now magical 'Luth Cievale'. The boy let go my hand, pointed at the letters, looking both pleased and relieved. 'Tak,' I said to him, 'Tak.' I had again to ignore his reply, which was surely courteous. He bowed, showed me a sign which might have said 'No Fraternisation' or might have been the street name, and turned back the way we had come.

"I rang the bell. Waited. No reply. I rang again. Waited longer. Still no reply. I looked along the street: even the boy had disappeared and it was beginning to drizzle or endamp or sleet or whatever that particular form of water condensation is that's so characteristic of Ardesh, and has done more to protect the planet from cultural invasion than any of the complicated strategies of the Trade Barrier. I shivered. It had been so glorious to get here, the hand written, brown-inked letters confirmation that I had found Luth. But of course, I hadn't found Luth because she wasn't there. It was too cold to wait very long and there was no awning to keep the precipitation off the back of my neck. Miserably I shrugged up my shoulders, took note of the address, hoping I hadn't made some classic blunder: mistaken the 'No Frat' sign for the street name. As I walked slowly away from the door, and the drizzle-sleet-endampment grew thicker, I began to appreciate why the Ardashi muffle up when they go out. I had taken it for a psychological response, sign of a nation of introverts, or perhaps a sociological phenomenon, a reaction to the 'No Frat' signs. Now it seemed imperative to keep as much wadding as possible between one's person and the awful weather.

"At the other end of the street was one of those intensely bundled Ardashi women, Kazbek fur up round her neck and one of those enormous brightly coloured scarves over her head. My ears stung. I tell you, I longed for one of those scarves but no use grousing. The Ardashi woman disappeared into a public console on the corner, whether for interpersonal communication or simply to get out of the precipitation, I had no idea. As I passed the plexibox I glanced in. The woman had taken her gloves off and there was something about those wide, strong fingers on the buttons that was very familiar. Of course. It was Luth Cievale. My Luth to be. I banged on the plexibox and tugged the door open against the rising wind.

"'Luth!' I shouted for joy.
She whirled, her face frightened and angry. Then she recognised me. We returned to her room, so I got to see the other side of that bland door after all. We sat on her bed drinking tchai and smetalaya. Suddenly Luth said,
'Let's go for a walk. I need air.'
"'But it's cold and wet out there. And it's warm and comfortable in here. I'm tired of dragging around this strange city where I don't recognise anything.' She looked me directly in the eyes and repeatd, 'Let's go for a walk.' I realised this was some kind of signal, though who she imagined would overhear us in her

student quarters and, moreover, who could be interested in our off-world gossip and flirtation, I did not know.

"We walked through the still deserted streets. One of the suns, don't remember which, did cut through the fog layer and dance off the pink, yellow, blue and pale green buildings and the shiny wet backs of the stone lions. I paid little attention to where we were going; I was with Luth Cievale at last and alone. I knew I must court her now with the utmost of my skill, I would not get such a grand opportunity again. Lust wanes too quickly with separation and I wanted a consummation right away.

"Out of the failing light appeared a large old building sitting in a piece of waste ground. The waste ground was unusual in itself as Ardesh is a small planet where every inch has been planned and made functional and the building, with its black stone, its bricked in windows, its jutting turrets, craved explanation. Indeed, the very fact that it stood alone, single storey with a high-arched roof, where all other edifices are terraced skyscrapers reaching upward, downward, outward, would set a person wondering. I turned to Luth.

"'Religion,' she whispered.

"'But that's banned on Ardesh,' I said. For even I knew the history of Lerrinsky and the materialist revolution. The Ardashi had been known as 'the people of beauty' or 'the soulful ones' before they were forced into the 25th Century by the realisation that their planet had a burgeoning population and a tiny surface area. Religion was outlawed the same day the 'No Fraternisation' signs went up.

"'It's a beautiful building,' Luth explained, 'The only one left on the planet. The Party decided they could leave one standing, surrounded by barren waste, as a symbol of the redundancy of religion. I like to think they each had a spark left in their souls, kindled by the knowledge that the building yet stands, and they could not, at the final decree, bear to extinguish that spark.'

"The black building was indeed beautiful. A dull,

13

formal colour, its straight, classical lines set off by the
flying turrets, the empty ground a majestic, swirling
mantel. Out of the gloom came small, bent figures,
moving slowly toward the door. They were covered
up, Ardashi fashion, so that no part of their bodies
was visible and so muffled even their shape was but a
mound of padding. There were no groups or pairs,
each figure moved as though in total isolation; no calls
of greeting, no salutations of the hand. They disappeared inside the black building, one after another.

"'Old women,' said Luth, 'Dead soon the Party
reckons. And no youth taking up the habit. All over
within the decade.'

"Luth gestured to a rock overgrown with moss so
that one guessed at permanent damp and no sunlight.
We sat down, our backs to the black building, looking
out over one of the endless series of canals, the light
scent of mint filling our nostrils, but whether it was
carried from the banks of the canal or oozed from the
rock we sat upon, I am uncertain. Then Luth spoke,
lighting up at the same time so that, now dark had
fallen, the only bright gleam was the red tip of her
cigarette as it moved through the air from lap to
mouth, occasionally punctuating the story by describing wild arcs and insistent dots.

"'I could not stay in that room any longer,' she
began. 'Ever since this morning, since I heard about
the boy, I have not been able to rest. I have tried to
work, to do my quota on the street-sweeping team, but
I know I can do nothing until I relate that story to
someone else.'

"'And you've picked me to be the one,' I said.
She ignored my banality."

Rennen flicked her eyes over Tutor Tet. No longer
making surreptitious notes on his desk or tapping
buttons on the console, he was entirely engrossed in
the story. She took an educated guess that he
understood Sing, although he probably could not
speak it. Fluidly Rennen switched from Gden to Sing,
as though to mark Luth as a Sing native, an artistic
desire to introduce local colour by a change in

14

language. Tutor Tet was listening avidly. Rennen continued with the tale, sliding gradually up the Sing mood register to Siren, lulling and fascinating Tet into passive audition. Rennen's voice was rich and full, a finely tuned instrument.

"'Three days ago,' Luth said, 'A boy went missing from a block of flats. A little blue-eyed boy. Only eight years old. Lived with his grandmother on the tenth floor. He had gone to school in the morning with the other children from the block. Many thought he had returned with them in the evening, but none could be certain: was it this day they had all played ball? was it this day they got caught in the wet? This day or another? They were not sure. The grandmother was wretched; the boy was all she had. Neighbours were questioned, the civil watch called, pictures circulated, the Gates alerted.

"This morning a woman looked out from her balcony and noticed a small figure standing stock still in the asphalt courtyard between the blocks. Fifteen floors off the ground it was impossible to tell was this a man, or a woman, or indeed a child. Half an hour passed. The figure had not moved. The woman called a friend from across the landing and together they went down to the courtyard. On ground level they saw at once that it was a child. Some paces nearer told them it was the boy who had been missing. They called his name and he turned toward them as though waiting. They came nearer. He stood still, facing them. Finally they reached him and saw why it was he had not run up to his grandmother's flat in his usual way.'"

Tutor Tet's face was rapt with attention. Rennen's rich Siren voice played on.

"'The little boy blinked unseeing. The cornflower blue irises of his eyes had been cut out.'"

Tutor Tet yelped and protected his own eyes with his hands. Rennen's voice whispered along the canals of his inner ear but he did not think to place his hands

15

over his ears. She had him exactly as she wanted him. The story was a success.

"'On the very spot where he now stood, three days ago, just back from school, the boy had been accosted by officials from the Party who asked could he show them the way to Nevskaya Prospekt. He told them as best he could, but they did not quite follow. They suggested he drive with them and point the way. The little boy had never been in a car before, only Party officials owned one. But he and his school friends had often stood and watched a car pass in the wide empty streets, crowded around when they came upon one parked in some public place. Many times they had begged the chauffeur to let them sit on the running board, though of course he never had. So when the Party officials invited the little boy into their car, he jumped at the chance. Nevskaya Prospekt was not far away, the walk home again would be nothing compared with the glory of sitting behind a windscreen, next to a real steering wheel.'"

The Tutor's hands remained clasped, blindfold fashion, to his eyes, anticipating the gruesome explanation which must follow.

"'They cut round his irises leaving the pupil intact but incising a large piece of the optic nerve. That little blue-eyed boy would never see again.'"

Rennen's voice ended on a high unfinished note, warning the listener to prepare for a breath-taking climax. Tutor Tet waited, spell-bound. Rennen, swift as a fish, smooth as the wind, fled from her Tutor's office and was away off the complex before he could leave the boy, and Ardesh City, clamber down from the heights of Siren, back through the entire Sing mood register and through to Gden where he could give chase. The quarry, when at last brought to bay, was not supposed to leap away again like a free beast. Tutor Tet ordered all the usual traces, searches, computer sweeps without much hope. Rennen might be anywhere on the Five Planets, or indeed, somewhere on the other side, Ardesh perhaps. She would be hiding in that big black church, Luth Cievale coming every day to bring her a bowl of tchai and a plate of smetalya. Tet played with the idea of organising an interplanetary warrant to search the Ardashi church. It would give him exquisite pleasure to bring the existence of such an ideologically impure building to galactic public knowledge. It would pour such humiliation upon the Ardashi Materialist Party. And then to catch Rennen, Gden national, Ardashi agent, seeking asylum in that church; that would be the crown. Unfortunately, it would backfire very easily if Rennen was not found there and by the time the warrant came through, she would surely have skipped planet. Fortunately Tet had other plans in mind.

By now he knew his quarry inside and out. He had proved conclusively that Rennen was a spy, and Differently Motivated, though he had yet to piece together all the parts of that fascinating jigsaw. Nobody spied for the money alone and Rennen, with her gift for total phonetic recall and signification, could have hired herself out to media, research or industry for five times the credit she must be earning as a spy. Clearly, and Tutor Tet knew this with perfect faith, Rennen was an Artist and her brand of creativity was narration. There was consummate craft in the story she had told him, craft which did not come from raw talent but many-houred grind. Tet's next move was obvious. He must write down the story Rennen had told him, as recorded on the tape. Not the ice cream sellers or the black church, evidently the centre of illegal organ extraction and interplanetary smuggling, but the tale of the blue-eyed boy. Yes, he would write this story and have it published in all the literary papers, syndicated galaxy wide. For a moment he wondered whether he should have it networked as a TV play. But it would be sentimentalised for a mass-market audience and Rennen watching it would find it so different in tone from her original that her authorial feathers might remain entirely unruffled. Tutor Tet decided to restrict himself to the written word. In whatever damp hole she was hiding, Rennen was sure to read it: her story with his name underneath. She would be unable to bear it. She would come. She would have to come and have it out with him. When she came, he would be waiting.

Rennen picked up that month's copy of the *Little Review* and read it in her lunch break. She caught *Blue-Eyed Boy in Ardesh City* by Tutor Tet as she glanced over the contents list. She skipped through the magazine and settled down with the story. Then she laughed. She was off the hook. Her Tutor had convinced himself she was Artistically Motivated. He thought she would come thundering in, risking her life to claim her art. But she didn't care. He could have the story; it had done its job. Rennen had moved on; Luth was now no more than a fondly remembered ache, Ardesh City one in a series of romantic settings in Rennen's past. As soon as she had mastered the cron daemon, Rennen intended to get transferred to Fortran; there was a woman heading a research team into shell who was, in Rennen's opinion, out of this world.

THE GETTING OF WISDOM

"You have four choices," said the wicked Queen.
"Three will kill you, but the fourth will bring you
happiness beyond compare. One of these doors leads
to a tiny baby, one to a handsome young man, one to a
group of women spinning and one to a ravenous tiger.
You may ask one question."
The young woman thought a while. If she asked after
the baby, she would become a nursemaid. If she asked
after the young man, she would become a wife. If she
asked after the spinners, she would become a worker.
If she asked after the tiger, she would become
breakfast. She looked around nervously.

"Why are there only three doors?"

"You have asked the right question," said the
wicked Queen, and a metal curtain swung down
between her and the young woman. "You have already
passed through the first door," she continued, "And
the tiger is loose."
Hastily, the woman tried the nearest door. Through it
came the heart-rending sound of a helpless infant
crying. She shut it again as fast as she could. Then she
tried the next door. Through the cracks she felt the
warmth of a fire, she saw a table laden with mouth-
watering food and a smiling young man with arms
open toward her. The heat, and the smell, and the
sight of the food enticed her, but she managed to close

the door before she was drawn into the room. Now she turned, in desperation, to the last door. This time she heard the familiar whir of women spinning and singing in high voices as they worked. One turned to her, fingers still occupied with the thread.

"What have you come for?" the spinner asked, "You can see we are busy."

"I am escaping motherhood, marriage and the ravenous tiger," said the young woman.

"I hope you can spin," said the spinner, pointing to a spare wheel with an air of finality.

For a moment the young woman hesitated.

"Close the door behind you. You are letting the heat out."

The young woman, hearing the tiger in the corridor, almost did as she was bid. But, at the last moment before the door locked shut, she caught sight of the tiger. It was yellow and gold, its mouth yearned open, its chest heaved gently, and its eyes licked the young woman with tender longing.

"At least," said the young woman, walking with turbulent emotion toward the tiger, "If I am to stay for breakfast, I shall enjoy the night before."

OUTRAGEOUS FORTUNE

On her way to the tube station Minnie dropped her washing off at the laundrette for a service wash.

"Be ready this afternoon," said the washerwoman, handing Minnie a ticket. "After two o'clock."
There was a sign on the wall saying that if you were in the habit of losing your ticket, you might like to leave it at the laundrette for safe-keeping. Minnie was folding hers prudently and putting it away in her wallet when the manageress came toward them bearing a well-stuffed pillow slip. This she handed to the washerwoman.

"Small machine that," the washerwoman grunted.

"Oh he doesn't want it washed," said the manageress. "It's all clean. He wants his socks matched."
The three women raised their eyebrows at each other. The washerwoman shoved Minnie's laundry out of the way on a shelf and emptied the contents of the pillow case onto the counter. There lay a pile of navy blue socks, possibly numbering three hundred, all bought from Marks and Spencers, and all exactly the same: same medium size, same medium length, same plain weave, same shade of navy blue. Each sock was like every other sock: any one of them could be matched with any one of the others. The washerwoman shook her head, looked up briefly, and said,

21

"Men."

"If they could behave themselves," said the manageress, "Like women. . ."

". . . They wouldn't be men," said Minnie and the washerwoman.

The Michelin was good, but the Baedeker was better. The index was clearer, it was easier to refold, and it included a subway map. It cost £5.75. Minnie was outraged. It most certainly did not cost that much in New York. A map like this, one sided A2, or slightly larger, of which the publisher will have pulled at least 100,000 copies. The mark up was astronomical.

Minnie was standing in the map section on the sixth floor of Legend, the biggest bookshop in Europe. It was also the worst employer. No one would stay longer than six months so the shop was staffed, almost entirely, by Scandinavians perfecting their English. The radical bookshops of London were staffed by Legend leavers eager to revenge their demeaning six months by spilling Legend security secrets. If you rubbed a magnet along the bar code strip you detagged the book (some said even a magnetised paper clip would do) and could leave the shop without activating the alarm as you passed the till. It did not work very well with hardbacks, on which the bar code printing and metal stripping was of higher quality. But a flimsy 70gsm map would not be any bother. Minnie's mind was made up.

She gazed casually around. There was no one but an elderly gentleman in grey flannel peering at a map of North Platte, Nebraska. Legend boasted that it stocked town plans of every major city in the world. Even more surprising than North Platte, Nebraska, classified a major city, was that someone should want to go there. Something of this unlikely circumstance should have alerted Minnie, but she was calculating which subway station you would want for Riverside Drive and feeling somewhat perplexed as there appeared to be at least six. The elderly gentleman glanced at Minnie who smiled at him by mistake. She was smiling for North Platte, Nebraska, but he was not to know this.

Once the gentleman was safely re-ensconced in contours and grids, Minnie palmed the little red and black magnet which had sat at the bottom of her rucksack since a Legend disaffected had first told her the trick. Holding the map in one hand, she rubbed the magnet along the strip in the bottom right corner. She would not, however, be able to tell whether this had worked until she had, or had not, passed the cash desk. She refolded the map, slipped it into the back flap of her rucksack, and set off toward the escalator.

It was not until she reached the fourth floor (Legend was built on the maze plan so it was impossible to descend from sixth to ground without zigzagging across the store) that she realised the gentleman was following her. For one half smile, which must have quivered for all of two seconds? Maybe he just wanted to buy his map. As she gained the third escalator, Minnie noticed that the numbers on the clock, one of which stood at the mouth of each shaft, were blinking on and off. By the time she had reached the ground floor, and was about to pass through "nothing to declare", she remembered the other thing Legend disaffected said about shop security: the clock numbers were used to call different store detectives to different parts of the building. Minnie had now successfully passed through "nothing to declare" without activating the alarm. The grey flannel gentleman was right behind her. Technically, she had not yet left the shop, and so was not, yet, shoplifting, though she had no business demagnetising shop property. Everything was horribly clear to her now. The gentleman was a store detective, store detective number 12, to give him his full title, and he had watched her demagnetize the map, hide it in the outside flap of her rucksack, the one not even bona fide customs officers thought to search, and walk brazenly through "nothing to declare".

The door to the street and certain arrest stood in

23

front of her. To the side was one other door and through it Minnie plunged. It led to Sugarfancy, the Legend coffee shop. On the way in, and to remind you that Valentine's Day was next week, there was a baby grand at which a balding pianist in white tie and tails was playing "Love is in the Air". Over his music stand hung his watch. On top of the piano stood an empty bottle of champagne, a glass and a vase with a single red rose. Water rots pianos but then, it was a rotten song though the pianist was rather good. Minnie felt fleetingly sorry for him. He should have been playing Chopin.

On the cake counter Minnie glimpsed a way out. She would pay for the map, a pot of coffee and a lemon meringue pie with the same cheque. It would probably have to be two lemon meringue pies: Sugarfancy accepted cheques only in excess of £10. Minnie ordered and sat down. The only free table was next to the piano. The grey flannel gentleman sat opposite her. She took out the map of New York; she was about to become a respected and even fee-paying customer, so she might as well act like one.

"I see you have a map of New York," observed the gentleman.

It was on the tip of Minnie's tongue to deny it, but the map now covered most of the table. She nodded.

"Are you going there on holiday?"

"No," said Minnie shortly.

The man was looking at her dubiously. She ducked into her rucksack for a tissue, a comb, anything and realised, to her dismay, and just as a full tray smelling fullsomely of coffee, lemon and hot sugar, was set before her that she had not brought her cheque book. There was nothing to do but talk her way out.

"It's for a taxi driver in Western Australia," she said.

"He has to know all about New York as well?" said the piano player after "Love" and before "Enchanted Evening". "That's steep."

"He doesn't have to," said Minnie, "He wants to. You see, he's never been to New York. He's never been to the States. But he's seen it on tv, and at the drive-in,

24

and he's eaten Dayville's real American ice cream made with double cream and fresh blueberries. . ."

"And real American oreos," said a woman at the next table dreamily. She had a pile of boring hardbacks next to her plate, the kind whose titles, gouged into the spine, assault one from across the room, causing one to wrinkle one's nose and demand of one's companion: "Whoever do you suppose buys them?" *Lolita*, *The Tropic of Capricorn*, *Beyond The Valley of The Dolls*. The mystery was solved: this woman bought them all.

". . . And real American Hershey bars . . ," said her friend from the middle of Germaine Greer's book about her father. "And Hostess Donettes . . ."

"Oh no," said the balding piano player. "You can get those at Harrods Foreign Foods, but not at the corner shop. I expect it's the same in Australia." Minnie nodded. "His cab is all over American bumper stickers saying 'Kill a Redwood for Reagan' and . . ."

"New York Dodgers pennants . . ." said the hardback woman.

"He has a pile of American cassettes for his cab radio," Minnie continued. "Patsy Cline, Connie Francis, Brenda Lee . . ."

"Bruce Springsteen," said the piano player.

"Dolly Parton," said a female voice from Germaine's *Daddy*.

"He has 'stars and stripes' patches sewed on all his knee socks," Minnie said, "Which take careful matching to ensure the flags appear on the outer calf. He works Perth International Airport to maximise his chances of picking up Americans and even, when he gets really lucky, New Yorkers."

The grey flannel gentleman, and the hardback woman, and her companion (who, having devoured *Daddy*, was now immersed in *The Memoirs of Charles de Gaulle*), and the waitress, and an elderly couple to the right who seemed at first glance as though they might themselves be American, but turned out to be German – their coats are, after all, too tightly buttoned – all nodded and looked expectant.

"Well," said Minnie, "This taxi driver tells his

25

passengers how he has always, all his life, wanted to emigrate to New York. He has never been there, he has no friends, no relatives there, and he has been turned down by US Immigration no less than fourteen times. He feels this to be deeply unfair. Is not his the most unbiased admiration you could find? On those lucky occasions when his fare is from New York, or at least New Jersey, he understands that's a poor relation, he asks if he could possibly prevail upon them to send him a map of the celestial city. Or at least a post card." Minnie very nearly adds that he has paid for such a map as many times as he has been turned down by US Immigration, but feels this might lead her onto tricky ground.

"At last the morning comes when he gets out of bed, fetches the paper from the front lawn and fishes for the mail in the crown of the miniature Statue of Liberty he has constructed to hold it, and there among his parking fines nestles a long thin manilla envelope containing . . ."

"One red Baedeker's map of New York," supplied the flannel gentleman, fixing Minnie with eyes which once sought to discountenance Scheherazade.

"Exactly," said Minnie, "Now, the taxi driver . . ."

"What's his name?" asked the waitress.

"John," said Minnie.

"Not very inventive" said the piano player tearfully. It was "The First Time Ever I Saw Your Face" next and that always made him sniffle.

"He is called John," said Minnie.

"John what?" asked the German woman.

"Bond," giggled a teenager who had wriggled in on Minnie's left.

"John Bond spends all his red lights, all his court appearances for non-payment of parking fines, memorising the map of New York. Finally he is ready. He goes out to the Airport and lands a New Yorker, first try.

'Orright then,' he says, 'Test me. I'm ready.'

'Test you for what?' asks the bemused New Yorker who has a few ideas.

'New York,' says John Bond.

The New Yorker looks relieved.

'I know every street, every crossroads . . .'

'Intersection,' says the New Yorker despite himself.

'So ask me,' insists John Bond, 'Ask me. How to get from the Juilliard School to Carnegie Hall. No, too easy. From Marcus Garvey Park to the United Nations Head Quarters, from CUNY to Wall Street . . .'
Obligingly the New Yorker asks. John Bond goes into full flow,

'. . . South on Avenue of the Americas . . .'

'You're making an elementary mistake,' says the New Yorker sadly and somewhat nostalgically.

'What?' asks John Bond. Perhaps now he is to understand why US Immigration turned him down so many times."

"So, what was it?" asked the German woman.

"Well,' answered Minnie.

"I know," said the flannel gentleman. "It's the one-ways. Those Baedekers don't show the one-ways."

"John Bond was wretched," Minnie nodded. "His world had collapsed. He didn't even have the heart to double park in his own street but pulled his cab right off the road and into the garage. He shut the door by means of one of those little buzzers like they have in the States.

"John Bond would very much like to have fitted his driveway with underground heating and automatic fans, but these were not to be had anywhere in the State of W.A. Apparently, so the salesman said — though what exactly made him a salesman, seeing as he was not prepared to sell anything, John Bond did not know — there wasn't enough call for such things, what with the annual absence of six feet of snow. John had observed that the leaves from his neighbour's citriadora frequently clogged his driveway and it would be very handy to be able to blow them away rather than raking them, but this had cut no ice with the salesman. There being, as the salesman was quick to point out, precious little ice to cut."

"Blimey," said the waitress, "This is too sad. What's he gonna do? Gas himself in the garage?"

"He should go to New York for a holiday first,"

said the teenager with the practicality of her sixteen years, "He might not like it. What if he killed himself and then found out it weren't worth dying for?"

"That's right," said the hardback woman, "He should win a competition. They always have a weekend for two in New York as second prize after you haven't won the shiny red Porsche."

"John Bond wandered aimlessly across his front lawn, there weren't even any citriadora leaves to rake. He found himself next to the Statue of Liberty, felt around inside her crown and pulled out a little padded envelope containing . . ."

". . . a flight on Concorde for two and three nights at a top New York hotel," supplied Ms Hardback.

"How did you guess?" asked Minnie.

"That's what my sister got," said the woman, "Only they should have said 'Three nights at the top of a New York hotel' because the lift didn't work and they were stuck on the twenty-second floor."

"Magnificent view," said the German woman's husband.

"So we heard," said Hardback, "Fortunately my sister'd had the foresight to stock up on *Caesar's Gallic Wars*, so they had something to read."
Her friend nodded approval from the depths of Pétain's Vichy.

"He'll be all pleased now," said the teenager, "That John Bond."

"He will be Over The Moon," said the German woman, "It is his Dream Of A Lifetime."

"He'll be pleased," conceded the waitress. "But this is what he expected. He always knew he was destined to go to New York. He's calm and purposeful, buys himself a new baseball cap . . ."

"Sells his house. He will not need it now that he is going to America," said the German woman's husband.

"No," said the piano player. "Where would he keep his country and western records? No point taking them to the States. American appartments come fully fitted."

"Only problem is: John Bond can't think of anyone

worthy of the second ticket," said the waitress. "But that's alright because . . ." She looked around.

"One of the other passengers wants the spare seat for her cello?" suggested Minnie.
Everyone nodded.

"But when he gets a taxi from JFK to his hotel," said the teenager, "He is bitterly disappointed. Not only did the map not show the one-ways, but it never mentioned how tall the buildings are. John Bond finds himself hemmed in by mountainous columns of brick and glass and the streets are so full of cars and people dodging them that the traffic cannot move."
The others appeared to be ruminating on this. Minnie felt a twinge of unease.

"No," the hardback woman was emphatic, "You can see the skyscrapers and the traffic jams in every Hollywood movie. Take Manhattan."

"But John Bond's only ever heard of one bridge, the Golden Gate in San Francisco. So each time the Brooklyn Bridge comes on, he thinks the film's set in California," the waitress pointed out.

"Yes," said the hardback woman's friend who was now flicking through *The Complete Works of D.H. Lawrence* looking for the good bits. "John Bond goes to New York and finds someone exactly like himself who has always wanted to go to Perth, Western Australia. The American John Bond has Swan lager beer mats lining the doors of *his* cab. They swap identities and passports. American John Bond uses Australian John Bond's return ticket and they both live happily ever after."
For a moment Minnie brightened.

"It is too unlikely," sighed the German woman. "This would never happen."
Minnie sank. The flannel gentleman was listening most carefully to the story's progress. Minnie's fate was now inextricably linked with that of John Bond.

"What's likely is that he'll talk the driver who brings him in from JFK into giving him a go at the wheel. He won't have realised they drive on the wrong side of the road over there; he'll take a left straight into oncoming traffic, the yellow cab will jacknife across the road, and John Bond will end his days at the bottom of the Hudson like many a New Yorker before him," said the teenager with the iconoclastic demolition impulse of Thatcher's third term.

Minnie glanced at the flannel gentleman. The seal was set. His face was grim. The nightmare Life in Death was him. But, behind him, glistened a counter full of lemon meringue pies fresh from baking. Minnie had an idea. It would not save her but it would bring comfort. If she was going to spend the next four hours at the police station acquiring a criminal record for a map, a pot of coffee and two slices of pie, she might as well order another slice. The waitress turned and shouted out the order, not wanting to miss the denouement. "Love Is A Many-Splendoured Thing" tinkled out of the piano. How the player had persuaded a baby grand to tinkle is not at all clear but it is certain that tinkling suited the atmosphere of depressed realism better than any grand pounding.

"Balderdash," said an old lady beside a potted plant. "Balderdash," she boomed. "What a generation of gloom and pessimism." She had before her at least three generations, but perhaps when you are over eighty it is unimportant to distinguish between one young person and another. "What hope is there for you if even in fiction you will not use your imagination? It may be unlikely. It may be impossible. But how glorious for someone to get exactly what they always wanted and, having got it, to enjoy it every bit as much as they always thought they would. John Bond flies to New York and he loves it. He loves America and he loves Americans. The taxi driver who brings him in from JFK has been looking for a partner for some time. He bought his cab licence from a contact two years before and needs to keep his cab on the road twenty four hours out of twenty four to pay his dues each month. He and John get talking; one thing leads to another. John Bond becomes the New York taxi driver he always knew he was."

There was a nodding, a paying of bills, a leaving of tips, a satisfaction of sighs and a going out the door richer than one came in. Minnie and the grey flannel gentleman faced each other. The gentleman called the waitress, flashed his store detective card, waved his hand over the table, over the three coffee pots and the three empty plates, and announced,

"Expenses."

The waitress grunted and jotted something down. The piano player struck up "God Bless The Child".

"I wish you continued success with your story," said the gentleman to Minnie. "At a rough estimate it has already earned you," he paused, "Twelve pounds and twenty five pence."

As Minnie walked through the automatic doors leading from Legend to the street, she had the eerie feeling that behind her back the gentleman was peeling off her suit and getting back into her practice clothes to limber up for the next performance while the piano player eased herself out of that itchy bald wig, scratched her scalp and combed out her long blonde hair. John Bond smiled girlishly and asked what was American for "tampax" while the German woman confessed she was a ventriloquist and had never been married.

On the way home from the tube station Minnie popped into the laundrette. A woman with a three year old had just finished folding towels and was on her way out. Minnie held the door for her. Fishing in her wallet for her carefully folded laundry ticket, Minnie went and collected her washing. Next to her a man was peering into a pillow slip stuffed with navy blue balls. He and Minnie left the laundrette at the same moment. The man spotted something, or someone, up ahead and sprinted off.

Minnie was reflecting that turning men into women was not such a reprehensible ploy and anyway what about Armistead Maupin who rewrote everyone in the world into a gay man, willing or not, when her attention was claimed by a woman's shouts.

"Leave me alone! Leave me alone!" It was the woman with the child and the towels. "I told you not to follow me."

31

But the man with the pillow slip would not go away.

"Please," he said, "Please. One last try. Make or break."

The woman had obviously decided to break for she picked up the child, who was at an age and weight when, though it is still possible to pick her up, you only do so under great duress, and hurried off down the street gripping the towel bag in the other hand. The man followed, catching her easily. There they stood a moment: the woman shouting, the man arguing, the child slipping, when suddenly the man hit the woman in the face. The child burst into tears.

Minnie walked up to the man and said,

"She doesn't want to talk to you."

He turned toward Minnie, eyes glazed.

"You must not hit her," Minnie insisted. Out of the corner of her eye she spotted a bus. With any luck the woman and child would catch it at the lights.

"But she is my wife," said the man.

"That," said Minnie, "Is a very good reason for you not to hit her."

The man stared. He looked distraught, but not as though he would hit Minnie. Minnie was frightened of men. A practical fear akin to fear of dobermans and rottweilers, which latter Minnie found it almost impossible not to call "langweilers".

"You should go home now," Minnie continued while the man was still somewhat dazed. She hoped to remind him of his school teacher; even dobermans had been puppies once.

The man looked round. There was empty pavement where his wife had stood. This one, Minnie, reflected, she might as well leave to Circe.

MANY PEOPLE IN LITTLE HOUSES

Heather arrived at the nursing home at her usual time, a bunch of daffs in one hand and a packet of her grandmother's favourite vanilla crackers in the other. The warden greeted her at the door and invited her into the study.

"I'm afraid she has slipped into a coma and the doctor doubts she'll come out of it this time."
It was what Heather had been expecting, but when it came the news was still a shock.

"Would you like to see her?"
Heather's grandmother lay in bed, unmoving. Apart from her pallor she might have been asleep.

"I've brought you those crackers, Granny," Heather said, "And some nice yellow daffs. I expect you'd like me to read to you, I've got the Daily Telegraph. The front page is full of that poor little girl, only three years old. You'd think they could leave the babies alone. I'm sorry, there isn't anything cheerful."

"Heather, dear," said a voice behind her, "You're only making yourself unhappy. Your grandmother can't hear you. I know what they say about people in a coma, but she's just too weak."
Heather stared at the bed and the empty person in it. She nodded, folded the newspaper and left it on the nightstand.

"Goodbye," she said, and went out onto the street.

She felt nothing. Later, grief would come, and even something like relief, but now she thought only that she had planned to spend two hours with her grandmother and what would she do instead? She knew no one in west London.

"Where are they all going?" asked an anxious voice at Heather's shoulder.

Heather gazed at her questioner a moment. The young woman had long lank dark hair, almost to her waist, huge breasts, a huge belly, stood four foot eight, wore a dark purple crimplene dress and the thickest, brightest green eye shadow in the Woolworth's range.

"Who?" Heather asked.

"The people," said the young woman.

Heather looked around at the busy street. There were harried mothers hauling children to school, smart business people hurrying to offices and indeterminate others popping out for milk or a newspaper.

"I don't suppose they're going anywhere," said Heather in the tone of voice the British adopt when they are being polite to the insane.

"But they've put their clothes on and gone out into the street," the young woman insisted.

"Well," said Heather, "Some are taking their children to school, others are going to work, and the rest are buying milk and newspapers."

If she had misheard or misunderstood, which was very likely, her answer was bound to make this clear. The young woman nodded.

"I'm going for a job," she said.

"Oh," said Heather.

"Do you think I'll get it?"

"I, I, well, I really don't know."

"The people," said the young woman confidentially, "The ones who are going to work, are they going to my job?"

"Oh no," said Heather, "They have their own jobs."

The young woman looked at her. The audience did not appear to be over yet.

"Um," said Heather, "What sort of job are you going for?"

"Collecting green envelopes."

There is no such job, thought Heather categorically. There is, in fact, no job this woman could possibly do. What has she to offer but ignorance and limited curiosity? Even as this thought formed another had taken its place: many jobs amounted to no more than the collection of green, beige or blue envelopes at the end of each week containing computerised pay slips, and many highly paid persons were gifted with less even than curiosity. Heather supposed that for the collection of green envelopes, the young woman needed no more than the ability to distinguish green from, say, purple.

"My dress is purple," the young woman said, for no apparent reason.

"And your eye shadow is green," said Heather, unable to stop herself.

The young woman blushed. "I'm going to have an interview," she said proudly.

"Are you going there now?"

The young woman nodded. "What's your name, anyway?" she asked.

"Heather," supplied Heather, "What's yours?"

"It sounds a bit like yours."

Feather? Eva? Jennifer? Beverley?

"I'm Lorna."

Heather gulped. "Oh well. So, they're both Scottish." Lorna looked at her severely but said nothing.

"Where is the interview?" Heather asked.

"Mrs Philippa Parker, Personnel, Room 101, Number 557 Sand Street, 10 am Tuesday 11th May," Lorna reeled off.

"That's in half an hour," said Heather.

"It's only round the corner," said Lorna.

"Not that Sand Street," said Heather. "It couldn't be. It's such a short street, the numbers wouldn't go up nearly as high as 557."

"What do you mean?" asked Lorna.

"Well, that Sand Street, round the corner, is just an ordinary road. There aren't any businesses along there. It's just a . . . a . . . street."

"They would need to have a street, wouldn't they?" said Lorna, "So that the people can get there."

Heather tried again. "But you want number 557, don't you, and there aren't enough houses in that street to go up all the way to 557."

"People live in very small houses these days," said Lorna, "Sometimes just one room and there's three of them in it."

This was perfectly true. Heather imagined Lorna lived in such a house. If you counted up the number of bedsits in those six floor Victorian buildings, multiplied by the number of people in each, you might find you had very quickly counted to 600. She did a rough sum in her head: six floors with three bedsits per floor, times three occupants per bedsit, equals fifty four, times two for each side of the road, equals one hundred and eight. In six buildings you would have over six hundred houses, if you counted each person as having their own home, which was Conservative policy these days.

"All the same," said Heather, she wanted Lorna to get this job, whatever and wherever it turned out to be. "Didn't they give you a post code, the people who want to interview you?"

"A what?" asked Lorna.

"A . . . a . . . a W number. A 'W', then a number. Like, we're in W10 right now and . . ."

"Oh no," Lorna interrupted her, "It isn't a 'W' number; it's an 'N' number. 'N22'."

Heather groaned. "Look, I'd better give you a lift in my car. This Sand Street is the wrong one. You want the one in north London."

Lorna looked at Heather dubiously. Then she said, "I can't have a lift."

"Whyever not?" Heather exclaimed. "For Heaven's sake. Your interview is in twenty minutes on the other side of town. You'll never get there in time unless I drive you." She thought of something and added quickly, "Look, I'm not a stranger. I'm Heather, you know my name. And I know you; you're Lorna."

Lorna considered. Heather hoped there was something in Lorna's brain which was even now telling her that Heather, unlike other people she might, and almost certainly would, meet, if she had not already

met them, other people who had somehow wormed
their way onto first name terms with her, that Heather
would not hurt her, assault her, rape her or seek to
humiliate her. Heather would simply deliver her, on
time, to the place where you collect green envelopes.
Heather wondered. Could it humiliate Lorna to be
helped simply because she was helpless? Heather was
offering a lift because she could, because she had a car
and time and, even, now she came to think of it, knew
where Sand Street, north London was. A small
compensation for all those she was unable to help: her
grandmother dying in a coma, the three year old in the
newspaper raped by her step-father, the heavily
pregnant woman on the tube to whom Heather had no
seat to offer.

"Okay then," said Lorna, and with dreadful faith
she placed her hand in Heather's to cross the road.

JENNIFER or The Secret of My Success

One winter's night by a blazing fire the woman who has everything was asked the secret of her success. Her questioner was a sad waifling who was poor and bitter and crossed in love.

"Your question, young woman," said the host, "Is not, on this occasion, impertinent but indeed remarkably apposite. I myself was, not long ago, such a one as yourself. I am happy to pass on the story of my success, which I hope will prove of lasting benefit.

"My fortunes changed in a dramatic fashion and the agent, or perhaps catalyst since the reactions she set off were more chemical than plausible, was Jennifer."

"In that case," said the waifling eagerly, "I should very much like to meet Jennifer."

"You have only to look," replied the host. "I had been sacked from my job after twenty years of loyal service, my latest novel had been rejected by fifteen publishing houses in one day. I was threatened with eviction by a property developer and my lover had recently left me for a young thing half my age. I decided to go to my friends and throw myself on their aid. I told them I was looking for Jennifer, must most urgently find her for reasons which I could not reveal. My friends swore to keep the whole affair a well-guarded secret but how were they to help? Who was

Jennifer? How might they recognise her? I explained that I had not myself met Jennifer in the flesh so could not supply a physical description, but the woman lived, or had at some point lived, in a squat in Brixton, was American with a New York accent. Next day the calls started to come in. Someone had found a Margaret from Boston who was now living in a basement in Islington, she was sure it was the right one, had invited her for dinner and would I like to come? I shook my head and sighed, it was a Jennifer I wanted, but since they had gone to such a lot of trouble, I would go along and meet Margaret. Next someone found me an Elizabeth from Chicago on a barge in Maida Vale; would I come to a small party? Still no sign of Jennifer, but I didn't like to say no. Next came a Catherine from San Francisco living in a penthouse in Chelsea. Cocktails this time. Then a South American Isaura and a Japanese Yukio Tegawa.

"No one came up with a New York Jennifer living in a squat in Brixton, but during the course of the dinner parties, cocktail parties, golf tournaments and boxes at the opera, Margaret got me a job as a merchant banker, Elizabeth secured a New York agent who sold the serial rights to my novel; Catherine sublet the penthouse: no rent but would I please feed the cat; Isaura fell in love with me and Yukio named the new mainframe computer after me."

"What about Jennifer?" asked the pedantic waifling.

"Never did meet her," said the woman who had everything, "Perhaps you'll have that pleasure. Perhaps you'll tell me what I missed."

LUST, AND THE OTHER HALF

The beginning of the drought in Jean and Rowena's sexual relations had coincided with Melanctha Adam's visit to London on a lecture tour promoting her new book, *My Life As A Sex Radical*. Rowena, assiduously practising to be young and impressionable, had got caught up in Melanctha adulation. Jean suspected Rowena's new interest had arisen in order to fill the gap which sex usually occupied. Jean had recently taken to supporting Stella Maris, Melanctha's opposite number, as it were, in the faint hope that a good argument might stimulate a good time in bed. If Rowena's dalliance with the New Orthodoxy gave her no more than an expanded vocabulary with which to discuss what she and Jean did in bed, or rather had done in bed before Rowena took her body away, that would be better than Jean's misgivings allowed her to hope for. In the back of her mind lurked the nagging anxiety that all this "sexual articulation", as Rowena put it, was an elaborate mask to hide what was really wrong between them. The words, the concepts, had been in common lesbian parlance for at least the millennium; the trouble was that Rowena could not bring herself to use them. She'd had only one woman lover before Jean who, Jean was convinced, was part of the problem.

Jean yearned to open her loving arms once again to sweet, succulent Rowena for a long night of mouths and skin, flesh and sweet, old-fashioned lesbian sex, the naked, woman to woman kind with all the fingers, tongues and tenderness God had given them, and without extraneous items like dildos, leather straps, sex manuals, sex therapists and kitchen sinks. All the paraphernalia which served only to take their precious attention away from each other at a moment when "paying attention" was the only possible point of the encounter.

"Melanctha Adam's such a goddamn liberal, you'd have your work cut out to make her sound even half-assed. Picked her name out of Gertrude Stein and never bothered to read the story it came from," sneered Jean. Anger always made her scornful.

"Melanctha is warm, friendly and charming," Rowena pouted. "You only call her liberal because she doesn't try to censor anybody."

"What's charm got to do with it?" snapped Jean. "She was speaking at a conference not a dinner party." Jean did not want to have this argument. She did not want to argue on these terms. And here she was, right in the middle, as usual.

"Talking of dinner, did you hear about the time Stella Maris got invited to Gloria's? They say she was worse than an obstreperous parrot, biting teeth and shitting on silk shirt sleeves."

"Melanctha on a public platform is like Donald Duck trying to tap dance. Whereas Stella has a brain the size of a satellite dish. And she has the strength of her convictions."

"So has Melanctha."

"There is no strength in Melanctha's politics. She's pro SM, pro public sex, pro paedophilia . . ."

"At least Melanctha's in favour of something. Stella's just anti-sex. Probably never had an orgasm."

"Neither have I," muttered Jean, "Not for so long I'm surprised I remember what it means. Must be a race memory."

Studiously, Rowena ignored her lover's mutter.

"Stella is pro-lesbian," declared Jean. If they weren't going to have sex, at least she could win the argument.

"Melanctha is pro-lesbian," Rowena returned, giving not an inch.

"Must be thinking of different lesbians," Jean sighed. While Rowena was busy regarding lesbian sexuality as a delicious secret only recently unearthed by the bravery of the sex radicals, there was very little Jean could say. No hint of judgement (and certainly no physical practice) was to interfere with the delicate unveiling process. If in doubt, you consulted a manual, not the woman at the laundrette, your neighbour, your lover or your own body.

"Rowena," Jean said, patiently, "That woman thinks sadism's just one of life's adventures."

"Oh I know," chirruped sweet Rowena, "But I've met some of those SM women. When I went to hear Melanctha. They're very young, you know. They were nice, held the door open for me."

"They were, doubtless, polite."

"And I saw this punk girl, about sixteen, very frightening to look at. In Piccadilly Circus . . ."

"Punks aren't, necessarily, into S and M."

"They wear the same clothes," asserted Rowena. "This tramp had a fit or something, right there on the pavement, and no one did anything except the punk. She stepped right in and stuck her fingers down his throat."

"Oh good," said Jean. What could she say when this innocence Rowena was so determined to safeguard was exactly what had attracted her in the first place?

"Rowena, I'm not talking about kind-hearted sixteen-year-olds. In California, Pam Fornica carved a swastika on her lover's shoulder. There are women who have had to have hysterectomies, women who are permanently incontinent and will need to wear nappies for the rest of their lives because of SM encounters. Can you imagine . . . ?"

"Yes!" Rowena shouted. "You always do this. Every time. You . . . you . . . you tell me things! Like that awful book, *Gynecology*. Full of horrors. You do it

42

to up the ante, don't you, Jean? Talk about an SM
relationship, what do you think we've got?"
Jean could think of absolutely nothing to say. She
might as well be throwing bottles into the sea, there
was as much chance of a rational reply.

Rowena stormed off to work, for which she was
already late. Every time. Every bloody time. She and
Jean had what seemed to Rowena a perfectly equal
exchange of opinions and then Jean would lift the
whole discussion from under her and throw down
something so hideous that all you could do was beg,
"Don't tell me about it." Rowena was tired of having
the wind knocked out of her. It was not fair. There was
Jean's experience of SM, taken from books, Rowena
suspected since Jean had never been to California, and
there was Rowena's experience of SM, taken from real
live women she had actually met. Two subjective
accounts, each equally possible, though Rowena's was
always nicer. And every bloody time Jean's version
won. How could you have a relationship with a
woman on the basis that she win every argument? And
if Jean really felt as contemptuous of Rowena's
reasoning as she appeared, then what the hell was she
doing in a relationship with Rowena? Was it Rowena's
inferiority which attracted her? Huh. Rowena wished,
as always, that she had put this to Jean while they
were arguing but, as always, she had chickened out.
Jean had more experience of everything than Rowena
who had had only one lesbian relationship before, and
even then she had never dared tell Jean the truth about
it.
    Rowena was cycling along the tow-path of the
Kensal Canal, past the new Sainsbury's and the lone
fishermen, the trees and tombstones of the two
graveyards casting thick shadows on the filthy water,
when something caught her eye. Only a very persistent, and very flamboyant, something had a hope in
hell of catching Rowena's eye. She was not so much
upset as shaken, shocked, though New Orthodoxy
people declared themselves unshockable. This something was so persistent that it followed Rowena's

bicycle, sitting doggedly in her peripheral vision. It was as flamboyant as a Champagne Magnum bobbing about in an urban canal. Exactly as flamboyant, for a Champagne Magnum is what it turned out to be. Rowena fished it out with distracted fury. Inside was a slip of paper. She found a lolly stick by a clump of balding grass, stuck it through the neck of the bottle, and scrabbled for the piece of paper.

"Every orgasm a wanted orgasm," it said.

Rowena, unused to being apostrophised in this manner by subaqueous anima, was a little nonplussed. Nonplussed is a thoroughly English state and Rowena spent a lot of her time in it. It is peculiarly suited to situations where emotion is required, but one is not quite sure which. Eventually, alas, one has to settle for one. Surprise would have been perfectly appropriate. Like a young doe, a lady may be gracefully startled on almost any occasion. Unfortunately, Rowena was not surprised; she expected communication from strangers. She had the sort of sweet, round face and small, chubby figure which inspire confidence and make of their owner a perfect best friend. Only the vehicle of this communication was unusual. Messages in bottles come from foreign shores and require painstaking translation from the classical Aramaic before the heroine can be rescued. Rowena had fished the Champagne Magnum out of a swell of old tyres, bits of wood, used durex and a bent syringe. The Kensal Canal is not the most romantic glade.

"Who are you?" Rowena wrote back on a torn piece of shopping list. Questions are a useful fielding tactic. She placed her message in an ink pot newly emptied for the occasion. One might sacrifice two fluid ounces of blue black for the pleasure of a new thought. Rowena giggled. How could you have an orgasm against your will? "That's like saying you can't have sex against your will," Jean's voice answered implacably. Rowena flung the ink pot into the canal and flounced back onto her bike, but Jean's voice continued, "Incest survivors have had orgasms when they were raped. It's just a physiological reaction." Rowena sped off again, riding straight over a fishing line in her anxiety to get away from Jean and her horror stories.

That afternoon another bottle awaited her.

"I am the lesbian who turns the page and makes a cup of tea when the sex scene begins. Why can't we leave our heroines to attend each other in private?"

"I think we should be grateful to the lesbians who have opened up our sexuality as an area of contemplation," Rowena replied primly in a mixed herbs jar. The New Orthodoxy dictated that in the bad old days lesbians had not talked about sex, thereby creating sado-masochism, but that all this had changed now that a few brave women were saying loudly and clearly that they liked to fuck and, what's more, so had their mothers. Quite why adult women had to call upon the shades of their ancestors, Rowena did not know. Evidently there were subtleties as yet beyond her. She hoped in time to sophisticate even those remote outposts of naivety still maculating her psyche. Meanwhile she was relieved to have an opinion and be able to trot it out as firmly as though she had coined it herself.

"Since when have lesbians not talked about sex, written about sex, dreamed about sex?" demanded the next message.

Maybe the message writer was unaware of the New Orthodoxy. Rowena decided to start small. It was nice to be able to talk about these things without anyone yelling at her.

"Have you heard of political lesbianism?"
The answer came back so fast, the bottle might have been waiting in the water before Rowena even threw hers in.

"You're going to tell me it's a theory that a lesbian is a woman who, for political reasons, does not fuck men. You're going to tell me it leaves out the main point: sex with women, lust, desire, craving, salivation. You're going to tell me all about compulsory heterosexuality and the lesbian continuum. Then you're going to say that the continuum belittles sex. You have decided to bore my pants off, which, I suppose, is one way to do it."

Rowena was nonplussed again. Well, to be honest, she was somewhat minussed. It is hard to have the strength of your convictions when they are on loan from someone else.

"What do you want?" she wrote.

"Debate, discussion, the clash of cymbalic minds."

"Fancy yourself, don't you."

"Now you're talking. How about a little verbal sparring. Or even a lot. Just don't give me any more clichés."

But Rowena had, at last, decided on an attitude. She was going to be affronted.

"I am tired of these damp diatribes under glass," she wrote, "I am a dyke of the nineties, I eat fast food and drive at a 120 mph. I'm excited by the work of the sex radicals because it puts lust back on the map. I read lesbian detective stories and have no dependents: not that I'm undependable, I'm just good at stating my needs. I never asked to be a lesbian activist. I want to be a secretary and rule the world like the others."

"Yeah?" came the reply in a fiery Tabasco sauce bottle, "Bet you call prostitutes 'sex workers' 'n all."

But Rowena did not stoop to fish it out. She by-passed the canal and rode to work by Meanwhile Gardens. She wore tight fawn trousers, the kind which look like tights which straight women approaching forty imagine will allow them to pass for twenty. The dyke of today is passing for a straight woman passing for twenty.

Rowena had misgivings. New Orthodoxy lesbians were, liberatedly, butch or femme, and while it was quite clear to her who was which in her relationship with Jean, she had become a lesbian because she was looking for someone like herself. What's more she had found one, and it wasn't Jean. That was the relationship she had had with Agnes, the one she did not want Jean looking too closely at. But it was irrelevant now; Rowena hadn't seen Agnes for five years. There was more to it than that; there was always more to everything. Things were complicated enough already without going into Agnes. There were some ideas

Rowena found it difficult to reconcile: sexual attraction was meant to be based on difference and yet what Rowena yearned for was the balm of like minds. Otherwise you'd sleep with men, wouldn't you. You couldn't have sex with a woman just because heterosexuals don't want you to. Surely the lesbian had to want to.

"Labia labia labia cunt clitoris vagina," Rowena chanted aloud quickly, and swivelled her chair three times to exorcise her blasphemy.

Maud, her co-worker, glanced up, gave her a considering glance and went back to her database.

Rowena imagined a series of New Orthodoxy penances: three labia and a vulva for suggesting that lesbian sex can be boring; a vulva and an anus for saying it in print; six hot wet throbbing cunts for not putting your hand up your partner's dress while dancing in a crowded bar. How many did you get if neither you nor your partner owned a dress? Rowena had always known she went about sex all wrong. Now New Orthodoxy had provided her with standards: lots and often; you can never be too loud or too public. Rowena began to write a message, not on the screen where Maud could intercept it, but on the back of an envelope.

"Can you be a lesbian and not like sex?"

Rowena gazed round for a bottle. There was a nearly empty atomiser on Maud's desk. Rowena took it and put the note inside. She dropped it in the canal by Sainsbury's that night while filling her shopping trolley.

The morning brought two responses, one from Maud, the other from the message writer.

"Have you seen my atomiser?" said Maud's.

"Elucidate your own paradox," said the other.

Rowena tried to settle to work, but Maud would fuss.

"Have you seen my atomiser? I'm sure I left it right here on the window sill. I always leave it there, next to the plants. Well? Have you?"

"What?"

"Seen it?"

"I threw it away."

47

"You threw it away? What do you mean, threw it away? Where?"

"In the canal. What does it matter? Don't make such a fuss."

"You threw my atomiser away? In the canal? Why? Just tell me that: why?"

"It was empty. It was practically empty. What's the big deal?"

"You don't throw things away because they're empty, Rowena. You fill them up. What am I to spray the air plants with now?"

"I'll buy you a new one."

"I don't understand you. You shout sex words to yourself, you've been late every day this week, and you throw other people's atomisers in the canal. What's the matter? You in love?"

"Probably."

"Well, do something. Consummate it. My plants aren't safe with you in this state."

Rowena nodded. This was recognisable New Orthodoxy advice. When in doubt: have sex; no doubt: have sex. Rowena wrote a note.

"You said you were the lesbian who makes a cup of tea when the sex scene starts, and picks the book up again once they've finished and had time to arrange themselves? Well, I sit through those films: 'Cunts I Have Creamed', 'Rise and Rise of Hermione's Clitoris', you know the ones, with the glorious parade of wet red, or purple, vulvas, and I fall asleep. I wake myself up snoring sometimes and have to pretend I just came like all the others. Reminds me of those movies by Chantal Akerman where the heroine washes up plate after plate after plate."

As soon as this was written, and before she could have second thoughts, Rowena told Maud she would take the post out, jumped on her bicycle and pedalled furiously down to the canal. She felt excited, as though she had just understood, or was just about to understand, something important. That sex without emotion didn't turn her on? No. She was immeasurably emotional about Jean, only miserably inferior. She sat on the bank and gazed sightless as a pair of black rubber flippers floated past. There was a damp paper sticking out of the foot-hold.

"Explicit sex amounts to no more than naked genitals and multiple orgasm. We are led so far up the garden path we are lost in the potting shed." Their messages must have crossed on the crest of a wave. Rowena felt despondent. The correspondence was exciting, and certainly romantic, but it had begun to feel like an elaborate game. Rowena wanted a person as well as a thought. She sat for a while on the tow-path, opposite the tombstones, and remembered what had made her a lesbian. She was not temped to write it down. It probably would not have made sense if you hadn't lived through it.

Rowena had slept with a lot of people, men and women. But what made her a lesbian was her best friend Agnes, and Agnes she had never slept with. Agnes wouldn't, but for Rowena it hadn't mattered. Rowena would have agreed never to have sex again if only she and Agnes could live together forever and be devoted to each other. Agnes was the first person she had met for whom she was prepared to give up sex. It was contrary to all New Orthodoxy precepts, but it was the unadorned truth. Rowena, in common with many basically untruthful people, had great respect for the truth when it suddenly thrust itself upon her. She did not know what to do with this new treasure except to gaze at it, turn it around, poke it. What had been so glorious about Agnes was the way she and Rowena matched each other. They had it down to a fine art: intonation, clothes, mannerisms. One could take the phone receiver out of the other's hand and continue her conversation, having not only the same voice, but the same opinions. It was too late, and too enormous, to mourn Agnes, and Jean was so different from Rowena. Was it possible for lesbians to be "different but equal"? Rowena remembered Jean's expression when asked her opinion of Rowena's new slimfit fawn trousers. It was not for this Rowena had become a lesbian; but if lust is off limits to soul-mates, how could she be a lesbian at all?

Rowena imagined a series of soft touches and

delicate gestures, appreciative laughter. If they could not be the same, surely they could savour their differences? As she trailed her hand in the water, breaking the perfect, perpetually changing rainbow of an oil spot, Rowena remembered the slow blossoming of lust, one sweet afternoon when she had surprised Jean by turning on "The Marriage of Figaro" and dancing, dancing, dancing. Alone, at first. Clothed, at first. And all the time kissing, and all the time, to the beat. Rowena's finger was slithering over Jean's devoted clitoris, hand drenched with one last orgasm, then Jean's hand inside her, four thighs parted, knees and heels bending, tapping, and Cherubino was crooning that she finds no peace and can't honestly say that she minds, when a woman with a shopping bag grimaced,

"Blimey. They tell you not to litter Britain, but they don't provide any litter bins."

"In Britain," said Rowena, "They expect you to take your litter home with you."
Rowena was tempted to chuck one last message into the canal, but it would be better to tackle Jean face to face. As she rode back along the tow-path she noticed an unlikely-looking blue medicine phial dipping up and down in the water but did not stop to fish it out. The phial bobbed on, propelled by a slight wash from a slow gliding barge, to be pulled in and unscrewed by another mysterious stranger who would read, with perplexity and pleasure,

"You are not my other half, nor has my soul a mate. But stretch out your hand and I will take it, show me your step and I will pace it, give me the favour of your faith."

SPACESHIP TO THE
GOOD PLANET

Five of them sit cosily watching the television, a lesbian sitcom, rare treasure, and it isn't even bad. Ella's feet are in one lap, her head in another. Nicole is making a fresh pot of tea. Soon there will be pancakes and Shirley will offer a teaspoon of her closely hoarded maple syrup. They will laugh and ask how she proposes to share one teaspoon between five. She will reply that they'll have more fun all trying to lick the spoon together.

The phone rings. Nicole, who is nearest, answers it. They do not see her face go white, the fear in her eyes, but they hear when she walks towards them, saying, "It was a woman with an American accent. She said 'The Jew-haters must die.'"

Penny and Jane groan and shrug. Such a household for trouble, only the syrup comes in spoonfuls. Shirley is on her feet, her arms round Nicole. Ella is about to check the front door, somehow she imagines death comes through the letter box. She has not quite left the room when Nicole turns to her.

"Do you think it could have been Miriam?"

The scream which leaves Ella's mouth is high enough to crack the glass of the sliding doors to the garden. High enough, but not long enough. Shirley cuts it short.

"Could it?" she insists.

"It could not," shouts Ella. "No. How can you think? How can you imagine? Miriam doesn't go around threatening women. It's as likely to be an Arab as a Jew."

"Of course. Arabs always address their death threats to 'Jew-haters'," says Shirley coldly.

The room empties, the pancakes are never made. One by one Penny, Jane and Nicole go (cocoaless) to bed, slinking away from the hysteria and rage which has invaded their comfortable kitchen. Ella and Shirley scream at each other until the small hours. It is a few weeks after the massacres at Sabra and Chatila. This is only one in a series of anonymous death threats to Lebanese, Palestinian and Jewish lesbian groups.

In Shirley's collective there is a woman, Farida, whose mother was murdered in the Sabra camp. The row between Ella and Shirley has been brewing ever since Farida's mother died, ever since Ella started sleeping with Miriam. There is a sudden lull. Both Ella and Shirley draw breath.

"I don't want Miriam in the house any more," says Shirley. "It's an insult to Farida."

"Just because Miriam's Jewish? That's all? That's all you have against her?"

"She's part of that Jewish lesbian group."

"Shirley, you and I are both lesbians, and we are both in groups, the only difference with Miriam is she's in a Jewish group. That's blatant anti-semitism."

"I'm not anti-semitic. I'm anti-Zionist."

"It seems to amount to the same thing."

"My friends find it difficult to be around your friends."

"I find it difficult to be around you."

"We find it difficult to be around each other," said Shirley, "You know, if we were talking Russian we could make that one verb and conjugate it."

Ella raises her eyebrow. Shirley smiles tentatively. Her Russian came from her father.

"What makes this so much worse, Shirley," says Ella, "is how much I like you. I just don't understand how you can have a Jewish father and . . ."

"This has nothing whatever to do with my father," Shirley bellows.

"I suppose he's still welcome in your house, then," says Ella, "unlike my lover."

"You were dead right when you said you didn't understand," says Shirley. "They murdered Farida's mother. Can't you see . . . ."

"Who 'they?' Listen to yourself. Miriam's never set foot in Lebanon. She was horrified by the massacres. Why do I even have to justify her? This is appalling."

They sit down and look at each other. It is appalling. Of all her housemates, Ella likes Shirley best because she is generous: with her time, her property, her passions, herself. Whatever Shirley protested, if she'd cooked pancakes tonight, she would have used up all her maple syrup on them. When a row was brewing, Shirley and Ella had it, clearing the air for the others.

"Want a cup of tea?" asks Shirley.

"Love one," says Ella.

Shirley fills the kettle, picks up the tea caddy and laughs.

"Do you know what they're doing upstairs?" she asks, "right at this very moment?"

Ella shakes her head.

"Jane and Penny have crept into Nicole's room and they're huddling round her camping gas burner, heating milk for cocoa, like good girl guides pretending to be outlaws."

Ella laughs. It is true. She has so much more in common with Shirley than with the girl guide cocoa drinkers. Shirley brings the tray over to the sofa and is about to pour tea.

"Apologise first, Shirley," says Ella.

"For what?"

"For suspecting Miriam."

"Nicole said that."

"Nicole said the name of the first American woman she could think of. She's just a twit. But you thought it was possible."

"It is possible."

"Shirley, I can't stay in a house where my lover isn't welcome."

"I can't apologise, Ella. I'd feel I was betraying Farida."

Ella is too tired to scream any more. She wants the spaceship to land now, right now, and take her away to the good lesbian planet where no one is anti-semitic, or racist, or even unkind. Where Shirley's generosity would always outweigh her stubborn, stupid loyalty, and everything would conspire to bring out the best in Ella.

Instead she is going to leave the house now, stay the night on a friend's floor and, in the morning, join the ranks of the lesbian semi-homeless. Maybe in ten years she will have been on a waiting list long enough to get the tenancy of a bedsit in her name. She will, over the years of six month short lets in damp, insecure basements, come to regard her moonlight flit as a heroic sacrifice for Miriam. The politics will be lost as Ella loses her home, her old friends, and her job in the move. She will depend, almost utterly, on Miriam, and soon she will lose her lover too. And then, will she blame Miriam, absent throughout the high drama except as the first American with a Jewish name to come to Nicole's foolish and frightened lips? This is not the best of Ella. It is not the best of Shirley, or Nicole, or Jane or Penny. And as for Miriam, she is only a name. A Jewish name.

Ella is about to stuff some clothes into a bag and storm out when the first deep groans of Shirley's saxophone come to her through the open door. The full moon bursts through the clouds, the house is bathed in blue light. Ella stops on the stairs; Shirley's playing ripples up her spine. The light pours down the stairwell from the skylight; a cello joins the sax. It is impossible, but the cello sits down in the kitchen to a duet of bitterness and pain, loyalty and loss. Ella hugs her knees and weeps. A soft breeze blows in the window, the light turns purple, an oboe wails. Ella closes her eyes.

It is no longer mournful. It is beautiful. It is like listening to the March from "Aida," the Gallop from

Orpheus", and "Stormy Weather," all separate and all at once. It is like reading a perfect paragraph of Bertha Harris, eating three mangoes and swimming your fifth mile, all separate and all at once. The spaceship has landed. They knew how to find her after all.

IN THE RUINS OF THE WORLD

Sometimes I know that the alien in the spaceship warmed me, balmed me with its siren praise: "You, only you"; that it paraded its extraordinary intelligence before me, its skill, its languorous licking voice with such a way of saying "woman" that makes me feel held and wanting; so that I, balmy, warm and wanted, would tell it the very thing that only I know, that thing which no one else suspected and so could not have, under torture, wrested from me, that thing which will now collapse the fragile roof of all I hold dear, now that the alien in the spaceship knows it. And then the spaceship will disappear from the radar screen, send no more transmissions, close down its receptor. I shall be left with that voice saying "woman", I, sitting in the ruins of the world.

Sometimes I know that the spaceship disappeared only temporarily from the monitor while it effected landing procedure. The crowds gathered, the door opened and there stood the alien carrying roses, armfuls of roses, red, raw and unabashed. It waited one rapt moment while the tumult quieted, gazing with eyes which promised everything in a million reflected hopes. I watched and listened and I knew that now, at last, yes I, only I. And the alien lifted the bouquet and threw it with easy accuracy into the air, above the upturned faces of the throng, till it spiralled down, falling, falling and landed at the feet of she who stands beside me. As she boarded the spaceship to fly to another galaxy, another timezone with the alien, she plucked one rose from the bouquet and tossed it to me, I who had first known the alien when it was nought but the tiniest blip on the far corner of the screen, I who had transmitted long and nightly, guiding the alien in. I am left sitting in the ruins of the world, between my fingers a single rose plucked from the bouquet of another.

Sometimes I know that the alien in the spaceship stopped here only to refuel on its lifetime journey to the planet of water and song, harbour for aliens from countless galaxies, countless timezones. It took no passengers. The roses are withered, the petals scattered and she who stood beside me stands no longer. Speak, speak now before the spaceship is so far out it hears nothing. "I will meet you," I say, "On the planet of water, the planet of song where both of us and all are alien. I want your voice, your siren voice, your languorous licking voice with such a way of saying 'woman'. I come from the ruins of the world; I offer nothing but my admiration and my love." The screen buzzes, the receiver crackles; faint, very faint are the sounds which arrive. They might spell hope or death or famine, but I transliterate as I can: "Come. I have been waiting for you, you, only you."

MARISOL McQUARIE II

Marisol McQuarie II picked up the infamous *Self-Help Manual for the Resolution of Deep Grief and Positive Adaptation* which her elders had left for her. She felt a mixture of curiosity and steely dread. The manual had been written by her great grandmother, Marisol McQuarie I.

Marisol II was one of the third generation born under the alien reign. Each generation, it seemed, invented its own mark of rebellion and today's youngsters were claiming names for themselves instead of numbers. Marisol II's elders, amused by the new naming phenomenon, had laughed aloud — some with not a little bitterness — at the name Marisol II had taken. They suggested she learn something of the deeds and reputation of this great grandmother who, they said, had been neither great nor grand. The woman had come to symbolise the basest collaboration. Was Marisol II sure she wished to carry that burden? Maybe, the elders advised, she should read her great grandmother's notorious *Self-Help Manual*, an extraordinarily vivid exposition of the mind of a collaborationist. This manual had been highly influential, if not entirely responsible, for the failure of mass human resistance during the aftermath of the alien invasion. Its publication marked the beginning of the movement for assimilation to the alien lifestyle and might, the elders thought, prove a useful history lesson.

Marisol I had been thirty years old when the aliens came. She, like 25% of humans on the planet, woke up one morning to find that her world had been invaded by beings from outer space. The other 75% of the population was dead — something to do with the sound waves emitted by the alien landing crafts. All but 1% of survivors went immediately into deep grief, Marisol I among them.

"At first I couldn't believe it. It seemed like a nightmare. Impossible. All my family, my friends, my lover, people I hardly knew, people I disliked, in one night all were dead. I felt like the only survivor. No one I had known before the invasion was alive after it. Except me. Guilt would come of that. While my mind refused to accept the endless, awful evidence of the truth, my body reacted to it by going into shock. I was very cold; it was the height of summer but I lay under two winter quilts to keep warm. I shivered constantly, my teeth chattered. I couldn't eat, didn't think about eating but moved, kept moving from one thing to another unable to concentrate for more than a moment at a time. I took no interest in anything, I feared interest. I could not sleep. I would fall down exhausted after nights and days of racing thoughts and fidgeting limbs. If I closed my eyes I would die, would disappear into the cavern of all I held back. Only my waking mind and rushing body could keep away my disappearance.

"The first days or weeks or months I couldn't cry. I fought to stay alive without knowing who or what I fought against. Something was happening, even then. Sometimes I noticed; sometimes not. When I lay shivering and terrified, waiting for sleep to devour me like a giant cobra, resisting with every muscle at my disposal, I heard a noise, a rhythm banged out on the wall or perhaps the bed frame. Surprised, I counted: 1, 2, 3, 4, . . . 11; a pause, then it started again: 1, 2, 3, 4, . . . 11. It made no sense. But at that time, nothing would have made sense except to wake up and find it hadn't happened so I could have tea and toast and go to work as usual. Nevertheless, that rhythmic tapping allowed me a kind of concentration, a brief relief. I wondered who was tapping, what and why. I had not wondered anything since the invasion."

Marisol II skipped the next few pages. Descriptions of grief are boring. Long descriptions are very boring. As one of the third generation to survive a cataclysm which killed 75% of the population, Marisol II had heard a good many descriptions. Her great grandmother's account sounded pretty standard.

"After the first morning, when the radio announced the news in a voice unmistakeably alien, and I rushed into the street, joining the crowd of people panicked and hysterical about loved ones who had disappeared, some from beside their sleeping bodies, I no longer went out, no longer listened to the radio, no longer looked out of the window. I kept the curtains closed, moving around my flat like a rat in a treadmill. I feared the sight, the sound, the smell and most of all the touch of aliens. As long as I did not see them, I did not have to believe. But, like all survivors, I had been assigned an alien of my own. Or she'd been assigned to me. I did not notice her because my mind was preoccupied with visions of the past; as though I could keep the old way of life alive by not admitting the present. I would think even of my father – who was a bad man – with appalling tenderness, miss him with acute sorrow, longing for anyone, anyone who knew me, I had no mind for seeing aliens. I might have inferred her presence: someone must be keeping me alive since I was incapable of doing it for myself, but existence appeared to me to hold no secrets; existence and suffering were the same, unquestionable.

"In those stories people used to write of spaceships full of bug-eyed monsters taking over Earth, the problem was ever one of killing them, befriending them, or learning their weird and awesome ways. But when 75% of your own kind is wiped out at one fell swoop, let me tell you: it takes a long leap to get around to aliens so much of all of you is taken up with loss.

"But grief is boring; no one stays in it longer than they must. I began to feel a certain curiosity, albeit bitter, about the world, along with an exhaustion of sorrow, a deep weariness with grief. The first thing I remember noticing which marked the new state was a sign illumined in the living room, 'You are in deep grief. You have successfully passed through stage one, shock, and stage two, disbelief. You will shortly move on to stage three, anger.' I was, as you may imagine, angry. Such an invasion of my privacy, this sign in the living room, with its flickering lights like a theatre board announcing a new play. But what difference when the whole planet had been invaded? The message did bring encouragement. It named what I had been through, told me there was progress, that I would not feel this way forever.

"I was struck with screaming rage and great energy, a torment of energy. I ran along the street lusting for death; to hack, strangle, mangle an alien with my bare hands. I shouted and cursed those creatures I had never seen. I smashed the windows of many houses, but no one moved, no one came to the door. The glass echoed a while and then even the sound was lost. I was still inarticulate but concentrating, vengeful. I could piece together the immensity of the crime committed, itemised evidence with which to indict the alien. The voice buzzed in my ear, the voice which had conveyed the news,

'Good morning, how are you? the weather is fine. Today is the beginning of a new reign. We, original inhabitants of this planet, forced to flee for our lives two millennia ago, have returned to resume our rightful residence. The sound waves transmitted by our landing procedures have erased 75% of your population. This is regrettable. There will, however, be no bodies to bury as we have ingested the remains in order to spare you wasteful expenditure of emotion, time and resources. Our research into your psychic structure informs us that 99% of survivors will undergo a period of deep grief. We will supervise your physical welfare during this time. Once you have progressed through all five stages of your grief routine, you should request an encounter so that we can fit you productively into the new reign. This announcement will be repeated at five minute intervals on frequency 600KHz.'

"I must have heard that broadcast near a million times and not listened through the blanket of disbelief, then blotted it out with fury. As these gave way to curiosity, I felt hunger. I set to look for food and saw that the bathroom cabinet was full of vitamin pills arranged, oddly, in groups of eleven. What kind of alien is it that kills three quarters of your kind but thinks to bring you vitamins, knowing you will not eat meals for some time? When I at last felt dirty and longed for the restorative power of a hot bath with plenty of bath essence, I saw that the rim of the tub held eleven bottles of my favourite essence. It looked extraordinary, that line-up of pink, oleaginous liquid. I laughed. A tiny snort, but a laugh nonetheless. And then I cried. I sat down on the rim of the bath, bent double. I cried not for the dead, the dead people, dead hopes, dead life I would never live again, but because those eleven bottles made me feel loved. A sensation sharp as acid cutting a vein, hot not bitter.

"Tears and snot poured down my face, the shudders which shook me now were quite unlike the involuntary trembling of shock. I let myself cry, feel the depth and tragedy of what had happened because here was something which was not tragic: the row of pink bottles, the orderly groups of vitamins. Like a woman who cries for the death of a parent only in her lover's arms, I needed to feel that the possibility of caring, of being cared for had not been erased in the general destruction. I reached for the flannel, dry and solid from lack of use, wet it and cleaned myself. Then I heard the tapping, 1, 2, 3, 4, . . . 11. This time it came from the bath. I did not know what to make of it.

"Many will call me naive. How could eleven bottles of bath essence replace my lover, my friends, my mother, the woman at the post office, the bus conductor? Rather than believing myself loved, it would be more rational to conclude that the aliens have consciences which can be assailed by guilt, assuaged by the giving of small presents. I should have stored this in my brain as a possible lever against them later. And the vitamin pills: a piece of ugly cynicism. The aliens, having once spared me, wanted me alive for purposes of their own: slavery, motherhood, foodbanks, experimentation, anything. Why was I not enraged by this bathroom full of trivia?

"It is interesting that the question of my insufficient anger has been raised both by humans, suspicious of my regard for the aliens, and by aliens, wary that I may not have fully passed through that stage and may have fury still to burst. At times anger would rock through me, and I would feel pleased, obedient to the laws of grief, a conventional pleasure at experiencing the right things at the right times. But I know my feelings then, when I saw the essence and the vitamins. I felt neither anger nor cynicism; I felt sad and loved. These were such accurate gifts, brought by one who knew me, knew what I wanted and needed. And I wanted at that time, more than anything, someone who knew me."

Marisol II pondered this. It seemed incredible that her great grandmother had gone over to the aliens, and convinced so many of her fellows to do likewise by the publication of this manual, simply because someone had guessed her favourite brand of bath rose. There was a piece missing.

"Later messages in my living room read, 'You have successfully passed through stage three, anger', 'You have successfully passed through stage four, acceptance', 'You are now ready to move on.' I was not sure where I could move on to. I was tired of the five rooms of my own flat where the food cupboards remained miraculously full no matter how much or how fast I ate. I wanted to go out but was scared of what might befall. The day of the invasion the streets had been full of panic and horror; the days of my wrath they had been silent and empty. It occurred to me to switch the radio to a different wavelength, in case it broadcast news of the alien culture I had been at such pains to avoid.

"'Lesson One. Greetings and salutations. In common with many species we, original inhabitants of Earth, have a formal greeting structure which it is useful to learn by heart. The following exchange will exemplify greetings between two beings of equal status already known to one another.

Mary   Hallo Helen.
Helen   Hi.
Mary   How are you?
Helen   Oh okay, you know. Not too bad. You?
Mary   Not too bad. Fine really.
Helen   Can't say the same for the weather.
Mary   The one still point in a changing world. At least the weather is reliably awful.

The exchange between Mary and Helen would be structured thus in the language of the original inhabitants.

0-01-17/02/05-27,911	0-01-17/02/05-27,912
0-02-31/07/10-84,110	0-02-31/07/10-84,110
0-01-17/02/05-27,911	112,021
0-02-31/07/10-84,110	56,199
0-01-17/02/05-27,911	$\sqrt{112{,}021}$
0-02-31/07/10-84,110	$112{,}021^2$
0-01-17/02/05-27,911	112,021

In other words, the first speaker gives her number, the second speaker responds with her own number. The first speaker then adds the last five digits of the two numbers together, whereupon the second speaker subtracts the smaller from the larger number. The first speaker gives the square root of the sum of the two numbers, then the second speaker gives the result when the sum is squared. Finally, the first speaker ends with a reiteration of the combination of the two numbers. What has been achieved is the promise of unity, the possibility of division, some interesting operations and a final assurance of combined power.

'Now you try.'

"There were hours of such broadcasts, and they exerted a peculiar kind of fascination. I never had a head for figures. I considered the whole mathematical system fundamentally alien to my way of thinking, and here was a species whose culture, history, whose very civilisation were based on a love of numbers. I understood that the 1% of humans who did not go into deep grief were themselves mathematicians who had longed for the day the world would be ruled according to mathematical precepts. It occurred to me to wonder had they been in contact with the aliens prior to invasion, waved a flag even, to steer them in: Welcome Home, the time is $\frac{0}{1}$.

"It was clear the aliens believed they had been driven away from Earth shortly after the completion of some magnificent and mind-boggling structures, the pyramids I imagined. They had taken their case, apparently, to an intergalactic council, claiming they wished to return where they belonged, and so were not invaders. This was an important point, it seemed, as the intergalactic council aforementioned had outlawed the invasion of non-hostile planets on pain of intergalactic trade embargo or, if invasion persisted, armed intervention. The council accepted the aliens' claim. No one had thought to inform the current inhabitants of Earth of the council's decision, either because it was not thought that there were any, or because it was not thought important whether there were any or not.

"Much of the information in these broadcasts went over my head and I did not understand its implications until later, in conversation with my live-in alien. For the moment I gathered that their physical manifestation was that of a cross between a slide rule and a trombone. They do have an appreciation of music and art, but their favourite forms are harmonic scales and architectural drawings. Many of you may throw your hands in the air as you read this and despair of ever making enjoyable contact. Let me reassure you, I failed my high school art exam with the lowest grade on the range. The examiner took my art teacher aside afterwards and informed her that my drawing of a spirit level looked more like a strawberry plant. If it were a matter of life and death, I could learn to draw a spirit level which looked like a spirit level, but it would be at best lifeless and stereoform and I could never learn to like it.

"The alien view of poetry and fiction may best be illustrated by an account of what happened during my first encounter. I was, they told me later, one of the first humans to request one. Many survivors went into shock and stayed there, cold, trembling and insomniac till they died, twenty or thirty years later. Others got stuck in a rage, lived a permanent shuttle between attacking the aliens and being punished. There are those who refuse to believe, who have occupied certain districts of the city, districts of unbelievers where a pre-alien lifestyle continues as though nothing had happened – except that they can never leave the district, never hear news from outside. I could have written soothing pap for the shocked, didactic short stories for the enraged, pre-alien situation comedy for the unbelievers in the district, for I am a writer by trade and could envisage no useful career for myself save the one I was already embarked upon. But I found I could neither ignore the invasion, nor write my way out of it. I decided to meet the invaders as a method, at least, of unblocking my imagination.

"I had no idea how to go about arranging an encounter. Does one lean out of the front window, hail the nearest object which approximates in form to a combination slide rule and trombone? Wait for the announcer to repeat the box number over the radio? Tap out random numbers on the wall and hope for the best? It was easier than I anticipated. The day I decided to request an encounter the light board in my living room blinked, 'You are now ready for your first encounter. Dress in such a way that you can adapt to any room temperature. The presence of aliens can cause susceptible humans to feel unexpectedly hot, or cold. The encounter will take place at your dining room table and will begin at 8 am. You should be ready by 7.30 am.'

"I wondered what the extra half hour was for. It

seemed at first a prolongation of anxiety but I was to learn that my immediate reactions often did disservice to the aliens. Soon, of course, I would refer to them more correctly as 'original inhabitants', but I must not anticipate. I needed, as it turned out, fully half an hour to compose myself for the shock of seeing a creature whose physical appearance would be so unlike any I had seen before.

"I made a pot of tea. I understood there was to be a ten minute break after the first 1¾ hours, but that would not be sufficient both to drink tea and go to the loo. I decided on tea now, loo later. And there was the alien, my alien, sitting across from me at my dining room table. I stared. Nothing, not natural good manners, not fear of reprisal, could prevent me from staring. It did look like a trombone, with mathematical markings along one side like a slide rule. It was inhuman. And the way it just appeared while I was pouring tea — chilling. I reached for my cardigan. There was no part of it which resembled in any way a nose, a mouth, a pair of eyes, though I could sense it watching me.

"I remembered the exercise I had heard on the radio about alien greetings. I was meant to start by saying my number, but I didn't have a number, or if I did, I didn't know what it was.

'Eleven,' announced the alien.

'Is that my number?'

'That is my number.'

'You're number eleven?'

'3-01-17/12/37-26911, to be precise.'

'Then it was you who . . .' Was it? Was it this creature who kept tapping out that rhythm for me with such patience at my lack of reaction? This creature who had brought the vitamins and the painfully accurate bath essence?"

Marisol McQuarie II closed the book. Why was it called a manual? It sounded like her great grand-mother's diary. At times she felt embarrassed at the strength of emotion recorded, a voyeur on her great grandmother's pain. Was one meant to read it, recognise the stages the first Marisol had gone through, the bitter questions she asked, then do as she had done? Marisol II skipped a few pages of the encounter and dived back in further on.

"'Just because 1% of humans greeted you as long lost kin does not mean the rest of us can adapt to a mathematical way of life.'

'Do numbers mean nothing to you?'

'I was a writer.'

'Computer program?'

'Fiction. I made up stories to entertain people. Works of the imagination, you know.' Patently the alien did not.

'Stories?'

'Anecdotes. Accounts of things which happened, might have happened, could never have happened. It doesn't really matter which. It's the internal working of the story that counts.'

'An internal equation where the values have no meaning outside of their relation to each other?'

'No. Not none. I mean, not no meaning. Some relation to the real world, but a vexed one. Necessarily vexed.'

'Why did you write? Why do you not write now?'

'Writing was the best of me. The best of me is gone.'

'As mathematics is the best of us.'

There was a pause, as for the remembrance of joy.

'There is also poetry,' I said.

'Poetry?'

'Sonnets, for example. Sonnets have fourteen lines . . .'

The alien began to look pleased. I am not sure how I knew this but I followed my coup up quickly by tapping out the stresses for iambic pentameter and classical alexandrine. The alien was excitedly attentive. It emitted a quality of concentration, I don't know how. It seemed to me afterwards that it was at this point that my alien began to believe humans capable of deep thought and feeling. Previously it had taken this proposition on trust from the alien theory bank but had accorded it hypothetical status only.

'We too have poems,' it said.

'Tell me.'

'This is an easy one. For large children.'

I will tell you this now, although I did not learn until much later, that 'large children' meant 'young children'. Unlike humans, aliens — or originals as I should call them — get smaller and more compact as they grow up, or rather down. They streamline themselves and their functions and by full maturity could fit into a human pocket. By this reckoning, my alien was herself quite young. I do not remember when I started thinking of my alien as 'she' and not 'it'. When we became friends, perhaps, but that was not yet. Not by a long way.

'1 × 9 = 9	7 × 9 = 63	
2 × 9 = 18	8 × 9 = 72	
3 × 9 = 27	9 × 9 = 81	
4 × 9 = 36	10 × 9 = 90	
5 × 9 = 45	11 × 9 × 99	
6 × 9 = 54	12 × 9 = 108,'	

announced the alien.

I must have looked so nonplussed it began to detail the finer points of the poem.

'Observe that the digits in each product add up to 9. 2 × 9 is 18, for example, and 1 + 8 is also 9. Further, the units in each product are in a descending but repeating series from 9 to 0 while, conversely, the tens are in an ascending but repeating series from 0 to 9.'

I gulped. Life with the aliens was going to be completely impossible.

'I know a story,' said the alien. Kindly, I thought.

'Oh go ahead.'

'If a 5 litre tin of paint costs £7.50 and covers 50 square feet of wall and it takes 2 workers an hour to paint 75 square feet, how long will it take 4 workers to paint 500 square feet, how much paint will they use and how much will it cost?'

This time I laughed. The story had everything: character, commodity, action and it asked important and pertinent questions. I expect the original story concerned spaceships and light years and I admired the way the figures had been scaled down for human comprehension. The alien generated acute puzzlement."

Marisol II skipped again. This anecdote of alien thought had been repeated so often, it was nice to know where it originated. Though when people told it these days, it was used as proof of alien stupidity and lack of imagination.

"'So tell me, Eleven, why did you decide to leave Theta-Omikron and come back here? After you'd been away nearly two millennia and got settled.'

'It's hard to explain to someone who has never been away from her own planet how different even the least significant details can be and how much that comes to matter over the years. Our mathematical system is the basis of our civilisation, as you know, the source of our greatest joys and triumphs. Our history is the history of mathematical formulae and their application . . .'

'Our history is the history of great battles and great wars and great feasts and feats of killing,' I thought to myself.

'The planet Theta-Omikron has not only different gravity, different mean temperature, different atmospheric composition . . . to all of which we adapted, as you see. It was several generations before we were able to stay outside the Tent (as we called our prefabricated, imported city) for more than a few hours. Of course, six generations after that we were unable to feel comfortable inside the Tent. But my point is that while we could adapt physically to these material differences from our home planet, we had also to adapt our mathematical system and that caused more stress to our psyche than any physical adaptation of the body. We could go on being and feeling like ourselves whatever the physical form we were obliged to inhabit, but our maths were central, crucial.'

'I thought the point of a mathematical system is that it generates rules which are fixed and permanent. Surely $5+5=10$ anywhere in the universe.'

'My problem in explaining is that you are unused

to thinking mathematically except at the most basic level. 5+5 is, as you say, always 10. But, even saying that involves the introduction of a new proposition, a new sign. We could no longer write 5+5=10. We had to learn to write 5+5==10; the sign "==" meaning "always equals".'

'Well were there some things which did not always equal whatever it was they usually equalled, or would have equalled if you had stayed on earth?'

'Oh yes. There were. π for example. We discovered to our cost, while building homes outside the Tent, that the circumference of a circle no longer always equalled $2\pi r$. Sometimes it did and sometimes it didn't.'

'But that's not possible. Whatever the circle is, those are the proportions which govern it.'

'How many times did we say to ourselves: "But that's not possible" in those early days? Later, according to the history of my species, we simply learned to live with it, adapt our system, and add the sign "(=)", meaning "usually equals but not necessarily". Even chaos was not what it had been back home.'

'Sounds like an American in London with the dollar fluctuating wildly, having to know the exchange rate at each hour of the day in order to ascertain the expense of any item.'

'Indeed. But Americans can learn to calculate in terms of pound sterling; they are not obliged to refer to the dollar standard.'

'They don't have to but some do. Even after fifteen years there's those still counting in cents.'

'Imagine the American having to make a mental adjustment not only for money but also for clothes sizes, food weights, water content, traffic regulations, social custom and bath size. What's more, while there may be general rules for all these new measures which she can learn, there will be random variations which are unpredictable and massive.'

'You mean she'll be buying an ice cream cone and charged three times the normal price and it won't even be a tourist rip-off corner like outside Madame Tussaud.'

'You begin to see. What would you do in that situation?'

'Keep a purse for unpredictables.'

'You wouldn't long to go back to the place where money made sense to you?'"

Marisol II considered this proposition. The aliens got homesick. Even after nearly two millennia they were still foreigners on Theta-Omikron. So they flew back to Earth. Fine. But why wipe out 75% of the human population? If they were so adaptable, why hadn't they slipped in peaceful and unnoticed so no human would know for another generation? Marisol II turned to the index to see what her great grandmother had to say about the deaths.

"'You had to come back, I understand that. But didn't you realise that the sound waves on re-entry would kill most of us off?'
Eleven was silent. Fidgeting, it seemed to me.
'We knew,' she said at last.'"

There was a grim expression on Marisol II's face as she read this.

"'Then why?'
'You had forced us into exile before. We did not want that to happen again.'
'No we hadn't. Our ancestors, maybe, though I've never seen any record of it.'
'Your ancestors exiled our ancestors.'
There was a kind of stalemate.
'Why so many of us?'
'We would have killed you all but our food ethics did not permit it.'
'Food ethics? What has this to do with food?'
'It is interesting you should ask. For you there is no necessary connection between killing and food. We do not kill what we cannot eat.'
'You mean the people, all the bodies which disappeared, you . . .'

'We ate them. Humans have many valuable minerals: potassium, iron, magnesium, sodium.'
I felt like a fattened pig, chatting to the farmer who observes pleasantly that bacon, pork, crackling and trotters are very popular this year.

'You're cannibals. Barbarians. We haven't eaten human flesh for centuries.'

'Hardly cannibals. We are not the same species. You eat the flesh of animals and have certain codes about their slaughter, protection, upkeep. But you kill each other without rules in thousands, millions, not to eat, not for your own survival but to prove you are right. This is the basis of your civilisation: I am right because I can kill you. The basis of ours is $5+5=10$.'"

And so on.

"Did I decide after this encounter, when so much had been made clear, that the aliens were murderous monsters worthy only of disgust and horror? I did not. I found them admirable: their ethics, admirable; their system, admirable. To kill only what one can eat, this is a good basis for morality. The two events of importance in their history which were not discoveries, inventions or new applications of mathematical formulae were their exile from Earth and their recent return: anomalies. How could we compare with our division of all Gaul into three parts, our wars of the roses, our Gettysburg Address, our Hiroshimas, our death camps?

"But it was not dry argument which convinced me. I believe ideological revolution rarely is the product of theory alone. I was swayed by a memory of emotion, and a recent discovery. Both caused in me certain knowledge, though not of an objective, quantifiable kind. There was that moment in my bathroom when I felt not anger or cynicism but love. I trusted that feeling more than certifiable facts. And now, when the depth of grief had passed through me, leaving a terrible, daily sadness in its wake, the only lasting comfort I could find was that of working out relationships between numbers. While I was calculating that

$\dfrac{\sqrt{2}}{2}$ was the same as $\dfrac{1}{\sqrt{2}}$ I was absorbed, content at least if not happy. My waking moments were spent, even six months after the invasion, on suppressing areas of my mind which obstinately presented pictures of past happiness. Since I had not used my calculating abilities before, that part of my mind carried no lost images."

Marisol II believed her great grandmother had recorded everything as she felt or thought it. That the aliens — she would not call them "originals" — had seen a use in that little book with its astonishing conclusion, and sent one into every human household where desperate people read it, searching for any source of relief from the wet weight of pain, the boring, sullen sameness of grief, was not her great grandmother's fault. It was probably not her great grandmother's intention. But the question remained: given the existence and reputation of the manual, and the disrepute into which the first Marisol had consequently fallen, could the great grand-daughter justify her assumption of the name?

Marisol II shut the manual with a frosty snap. Immediately she reopened it and turned to the title page: *Self-Help Manual for the Resolution of Deep Grief and Positive Adaptation.* Was that the title Marisol I had given it? Beneath this, and in a much smaller face, was a dedication Marisol II had not noticed before.

"For my live-in alien, the mad woman in the attic. With thanks for the vitamins. I took them. They kept me alive."

Marisol II felt as her great grandmother had felt sitting on the rim of the bath, suddenly seeing the eleven bottles of vitamins, the eleven bottles of bath essence, which had been there all along. There was an almost fatal trustfulness about Marisol I, an optimism in spite of, in the teeth of tragedy.

"Collaborationist?" snorted the great grand-daughter, "Those dimwitted fools. My namesake was the last of the Romantics."

Marisol II made up her mind. She would take the name, and all its history: add to it her own joys and her own horrors.

"My name is Marisol," she said aloud, "Marisol II." The elders nodded and the aliens took note when she made her announcement, but each side remembered only that she was to be called in future, "Number Two" instead of "Number Eleven".

PLAYERS IN THE OBERLIN

At last she heard the sound of chimes, xylophones, pipes, vases and a two string violin. All the instruments played the same three notes, over and over again, but each to a different rhythm. A heterophonic web of rhythmic variety. She always entered the Oberlin by the same port, the place she had first encountered it: swimming up through the cavernous tunnel of the four-wide escalators which swept passengers out of the Piccadilly Line and into the street at Holborn Station. As soon as she stepped onto the bottom of the escalator, and gazed up at the rounded ceiling a hundred feet above her, she began to feel as though she had dived into water and was now surfacing, slowly, from the green depths of the ceramic tiled underground into a new world above. She would begin to move her arms in a dazed but vigorous breaststroke, watching the light filter down to her through the hundred feet of water. As she swam, way above the heads of the ant-passengers, they seemed to her a mere pretext, a flimsy one at that, for this majestic architecture.

The trip to Holborn Underground Station took place every Friday evening as soon as Madeleine had finished work. So that her friends would not become anxious, or suspicious about such a regular commitment, nor surprised that it caused her to sleep through Saturday and exhibit symptoms of transcontinental jet lag, Madeleine had invented a long distance lover, an air stewardess some took it upon themselves to decide, who was only in London on Friday nights. Madeleine's glowing, satisfied face on Sundays, her pinched anxiety on Friday afternoons, did much to add credence to the tale.

Madeleine hated delay. It was hard enough manufacturing a solid ten hour break each week without losing precious minutes for the airwaves to clear, or whatever it was. She had scant idea of the technical processes involved in her participation in the Oberlin. Were it possible, she would never leave but stay on through concert after concert, feeding on music and euphoria. But one could not live in the Oberlin. Not that there was insufficient to sustain her; there was plenty of everything any organism needed. One had, however, to remain grounded in one's autochthonous world; if one began to feel even slightly distant, then one's playing suffered. The Oberlin, the incredible music possible and continual in the Oberlin – incredible because unless one played it, one could not believe in it – was composed of passion, all the passion the players brought with them. If they had no feeling to offer the music, then they could not be part of it.

As she swam toward the sound, her body once again being absorbed in the myriad, burgeoning rhythms with only the pattern of the three notes to keep her from disintegrating, that pattern a safety net of steel and gossamer, Madeleine imagined a life in which the Oberlin played no part. A thought she could not bear to entertain at any other moment of the week, moments when the Oberlin seemed indeed like the glorious, impossible yearning of a lost dream. Only when she felt her re-entry secure, knew with the absolute confidence of an orgasm about to burst and rock her body, that she was even then becoming part of the Oberlin, could she imagine – since it no longer seemed like a memory – the life of a being deprived of even the knowledge of grace, a being living in a cave, with eyes upon its face but no knowledge that outside the cave shines the light.

What was the Oberlin? It was an instrument, or rather an orchestra composed of wind, percussion, strings; made of clay, wood, hide, bark, metal: all and every material found on the autochthonous world of all and every player: any scrap or shape naturally occurring, or manufactured, which could be scraped, banged, blown had been, in its time, an instrument of the Oberlin. Or rather, the Oberlin was the instrument and the orchestra and the musicians and the music: the played and the player and the play. Each instrument was played by a different sentient but it was the rhythm which varied, not the melody. To ears tuned to melodic variation it could sound monotonous, except that it had no audience. To hear it one must play it, be part of it and to be part of the Oberlin was bliss, and one does not say of bliss that it is monotonous. One does not say anything at all. The rhythms were improvised according to complicated rules which the musicians spent their lives learning from each other. Often it was conducted by the two string violin, but not necessarily. One had to concentrate utterly to know which instrument was conducting, and when. There was no written music, each performance was entirely improvised, according to the rules; each musician needed a keen sense of all the other rhythms going, she could not simply perfect her own piece. That would not have made sense, any more than a single note makes sense on its own.

When trying to describe the experience, players would say it was profoundly religious, religious ecstasy, because they were at one with the whole, they belonged and were equal to the consciousness of all the other sentients which made up the whole. Madeleine described it as like walking out of the bank where she worked and swimming in the sea, part of the waves, reminded that her body was nine tenths water and so was returning to its natural element. But then, each was describing the Oberlin to someone who already knew it; no one who did not know the Oberlin could understand the extreme joy of no longer being oneself, locked into one body, that this was not a giving up, a diminution, but an aggrandisement of the most selfless, self-conscious kind. A communion. And those who did not already know the Oberlin would shy away from the religious overtones of the experience, bridle at terms like "ecstasy" and "communion". But if one must compare music to anything, if one needs metaphor even at such a time as the word has been made flesh, ones own flesh, then only the metaphors of religion will do.

The Oberlin served a different function for the variously sentient beings who took part in it. For Madeleine it was a force for female liberation. As an Earth autochthone she had to find ten free hours playing time since, unlike more sophisticated sentients from other worlds, she could not simply "take time out" for the Oberlin and return to daily life at the hour the concert started. She had hoped to learn that technique but for the moment another problem loomed so large that she feared it would affect her playing. Of course everything affected her playing, and it was right that it should, but she had thought this might prevent her from reaching her entry port.

As she surfaced, at last, into the three note melody, Madeleine cried out,

"The Oberlin has been discovered by those who would harm it."

Like the resolution of a solid in a photograph where the darker patches stand out not because they are black, but because the whole picture is composed of a pattern of dots and there are simply more of these dots in the darker areas, so the Oberlin was a matter of degree. A fast movement was merely faster than a slow movement; pitch only that quality of a sound which depends on the rapidity of the vibrations producing it, and even perfect pitch is a convention relating to an agreed scale. Madeleine wanted absolutes, not degrees, and this was why she was unable to "take time out" for the Oberlin. Her desire for the absolute made relative time impossible for her. It was, she had discovered after meeting sentients from other worlds, a very human failing. She understood the Oberlin in her fashion, but her passion was for the absolute.

When Madeleine cried out, "The Oberlin has been discovered by those who would harm it", the triangle, who was at that moment conducting, took up her cry, fashioning it first into fingers (as Madeleine called them, after the three joints in her own; in search of new nomenclature humans commonly refer to their own physical form): trisyllabic sections, which were, in this case, a trochee followed by three amphibrachs:

Th'Ōbĕrlīn's / dĭscŏvĕred / bȳ thōse whŏ /
wŏuld hārm ĭt /

and then playing it out on the three notes possible from a triangle. This, and all the anguish which formed it, became part of all the other rhythms and emotions at that moment issuing from, and embodying, the Oberlin.

It is entirely unnecessary to know the rules of classical prosody, the words and ways of classifying stresses, to understand the importance of the Oberlin. It is difficult to imagine the kind of music played and the above serves only as an example of the complexity created. The human body sustains many more rhythms, on much more complicated patterns, without anyone ever troubling themselves to doubt the existence of the body.

And now all is revealed. The reason for Madeleine's anguish is entirely comprehensible. Isn't it? We, I should say I, for I am Madeleine who declares my anguish comprehensible, have taken some pains to explain the importance, the joy, the bliss, the rapture, the ecstasy, the communion of the Oberlin in terms which may be close enough to your own experience because I need you to understand my anguish. I declare it comprehensible to encourage you. If I had any reason to suppose you, any one of you, had yourself played in the Oberlin, I would say nothing. We would smile, and we would know. But I know that you have not, any one of you, played the Oberlin because the Oberlin is no more. "The Oberlin has been discovered by those who would harm it."

As soon as I broke the news and the triangle broke the news into fingers and added its tune, I knew the Oberlin was gone. And now I tell my story on the London Underground though I can no longer swim through the hundred feet of water which surges up from the Piccadilly Line at Holborn Station.

"But I do not follow. I do not understand."
Does someone say that? An admission of absence (understanding) and a belief in presence (explanation). Then I will tell you. You, I will tell. In my zeal to be understood I have described the Oberlin in terms of religion, in terms of music (which it, properly, is) and, passingly, in terms of sex. I have committed an omission, a sin which contains its own punishment: by omitting one metaphor I have deprived myself of your understanding. I said earlier that for Madeleine the Oberlin was a force for female liberation. I trembled as I said it and hoped that it would pass as background, subliminal advertising expected in a post-feminist age. But it was the reason for . . . everything.

Madeleine created a fantasy lover to allow her ten free, unquestioned hours a week, but this was no chance pretext: Madeleine wanted a revolution like a lover. She looked around her on the tube trains and she saw the same pieces of the same bodies dismembered and clothed in artifacts with price tags attached; she saw the same arms heavy on the same shoulders; the same persons burdened with the whole emotional care of other persons identifiable by sex, for sex is a hard fact as well as a metaphor, dividing the world as cleanly as it unites in the Oberlin, meaning the opposite for heterosexuals than for homosexuals: for the one: difference; for the other: communion.

And now all is revealed. The reason for Madeleine's anguish is entirely comprehensible: the Oberlin was only ever played by women, it was an enormous pan-galactic orgy. Would you too not suffer a certain sense of . . . loss if you had once been involved in an enormous pan-galactic orgy with sentients so different from yourself that all that was common was the fact that on your autochthonous

81

planet you served the function of woman, and made love just like a woman?

"But you are now describing the Oberlin as an interplanetary Women's Liberation Movement. Though we find the term rather, shall we say, old hat, still we were led to believe that it was a movement for women. You said yourself, you said, 'The Oberlin was only ever played by women'. Women, you said, not lesbians."

And I knew then, what I had already known, that the Oberlin was no more and that no one would ever understand my anguish.

And so you see that Madeleine's very human belief in absolutes, in this case an absolute and timeless incomprehension, caused her to fall back from the Oberlin and into the mouth of the tube tunnel, plummeting to certain death a hundred feet below, her body broken on the green ceramic tiles. For at the point of orgasm one does not imagine the absence of orgasm, as one does not imagine silence when listening to twelve flawless sopranos, as one does not imagine despair when filled with religious ecstasy. For the Women's Liberation Movement, as well as everything else it is, is a work of the imagination and to imagine it gone, to believe it might never have existed, that there are no others to take up the burden and the joy, is to sing it to certain death.

THE PROMISED LAND RECEDES
INTO A GREY HORIZON

The prospect of one, possibly two, months in Western Australia looking after her mother failed to thrill Theda Kyrannidis.

But it would put useful distance between her and Ranier. Ranier was Theda's guilty secret. Her guilty, gorgeous, cunt-melting secret. At first content to be where Ranier was, to talk to Ranier about the free radicals in the carbon chain, Rita Hayworth in *Gilda*, magic realism in the modern lesbian novel, whatever she could think of to keep Ranier interested, Theda felt things had come to a head the day she called Ranier's ansaphone three times during the day, when she knew Ranier would be out, just to have Ranier's voice to herself for three times thirty-two seconds. Theda had blushed the last time she had seen Ranier. Ranier, quite reasonably, had asked why. It was impossible to explain that she had been gazing at Ranier, because Ranier was goddamn gorgeous, everyone said that, and even Ranier described herself as charming; that she, Theda, had been gazing when Ranier caught her eye and looked back at her, and that there had been an annoyed, or annoyable, something in Ranier's look which made Theda think that maybe Ranier thought that she, Theda, was only staring at Ranier's fat, for it was true that Ranier was magnificently fat, as well as magnificent. So Theda had blushed and been quite unable to explain. Utterly aware that good lesbians do not fall in love, that falling is selfish, takes no account of the other save as involuntary catcher, Theda had proceeded, against all the messages her brain could feed her, to fall in love with Ranier. Next time Theda ventured to ring at an hour when Ranier might be home. Ranier said it was nice to hear Theda's voice. Theda asked how Ranier was and Ranier said she'd just had a root canal and Theda asked was that teeth. Then Theda said it, what was on her mind; "love," she had said, and "fallen," and there was an "I" which referred to herself, and a "you" which referred to Ranier. Ranier said, kindly, that all this was very interesting but did not have anything to do with her and anyway she had two lovers already. Maybe she and Theda could see each other once Theda had fallen out of love again; Ranier made it a policy never to sleep with anyone in the grip of an infatuation. In the meantime if Theda came across any good lesbian novels in the magic realist mode, maybe she could leave the details on Ranier's ansaphone. Theda, accustomed to a more intimate relationship with Ranier's ansaphone, declined. And fled.

Arranging leave of absence from work, and someone to feed the plants and water the goldfish, Theda set about the more difficult, but ultimately more rewarding task of finding lesbians in Perth. Her mother would suggest she join the Women's Cricket Club. Her mother had been promoting the Cricket Club as a cure for every female malady of the last twenty five years, from menstrual cramps and adolescent spots to hot flashes and single blessedness. As lesbians, like God, are everywhere, they are most certainly at the local cricket game. Theda had, however, only a month or two to find them and thought it swifter to try the places which called themselves lesbian. It is a well known fact that like calls to like, when they advertise their calling. Theda would need dyke sustenance if she was to stay with her mother, and the episode with Ranier had left her needier than ever. She asked around, wrote to any addresses which seemed likely, bought a copy of *Lesbian Network* at the Feminist

Bookshop and scanned every page. She learned an awful lot more about Sydney than her well-regulated life with its familiar corners had given her cause to discover: late night lesbian laundromats, hotels with "homosexual doubles", but precious little for Perth. There was one café, which had recently closed down; one corner of a progressive bookshop; one pub which hosted a women's night once a month: it didn't mention which night although, fortunately, it did manage to let slip which pub.

Either everyone was in Sydney (at the late night laundromat?) or everyone in Perth had moved house, because none of the friends of friends, ex-lovers' ex-lovers, Perth dykes who'd come to Sydney to protest the bicentennial, replied to Theda's letters. Nor did they speak to her ansaphone. The only lesbian clues Theda was to carry with her on the three day bus trip across the Nullarbor Desert were the closed café, the once a month pub and the odd shadow in the straight bookshop. Luckily Theda was very determined, and a few days at her mother's, passionately though she loved her, was going to make her very desperate.

Only poor people and English tourists travel by bus. Theda would have driven, had not her licence been suspended for a year, punishment for never, but never, paying parking fines. She would have flown, had her boss not refused to pay her in absentia. She settled in the long, slightly raised seat at the back and indulged in her favourite pursuit: dyke-spotting. It was a habit, it took Theda's mind off Ranier, and there was always the chance that someone on the bus could introduce her to the Perth lesbian community.

The only people she could cross off immediately were the men, but there were very few of them; all others were subjected to itemised examination at the first filling station. The Aboriginals sat apart, away from the roadhouse. The women pulled a picnic out of enormous baskets. Theda liked to imagine all five were dykes, so loud, so boisterous, so affectionate were they. She had to give it up when they launched into animated complaint about their respective men. There were schoolgirls bickering, which could as well mean sisters as lovers. There was another Greek woman, of whom Theda had had high hopes, ogling the back of her head on the bus. She had very short hair and no ring on her third finger, but she looked unswervingly straight, smiled so consistently, dressed so correctly, adjusted her make-up so carefully, would not drink tea with smudged lipstick. There were three elderly white women who asked politely why Theda was going to Perth and offered sympathy for her mother's accident. Theda felt the familiar *frisson* of culpable complicity in accepting the sympathy due the devoted daughter while concealing the broken heart of the spurned lesbian.

Where was the look, the open interest which comes from any age and any race, but always dyke to dyke? It was only when cut off from her lesbian homeland that Theda prized the thousand small signals of lesbian recognition. And soon a heterosexual drama was enacted before the whole coach, of such stirring pathos that it established this transit as a home-from-home for hets, pushing Theda even further into the never never.

A very small toddler trotted round the corner. She was dressed only in a man's shirt, the arms rolled up and the tail threatening to trip her at each step.

"Poor little mite," said one of the elderly women, "that fella oughta be horse-whipped."

"Calls himself a father," added another.

"Ronnie," called the toddler's mother, "Come here you. Come and look at the cockies."

But Ronnie was not interested in cockatoos. She ran toward the Aboriginal group where three children were tucking into ham roll and chips. She hovered on the outside, ogling the chips.

"Go on," said an old Aboriginal woman, "let the kid have one."

Ronnie grabbed a handful and wolfed them down.

"Hungry aren't ya?" said one of the younger women, looking at Ronnie's flapping shirt and bare feet. Ronnie nodded. Soon both she and her mother were sitting in the middle of the Aboriginal group sharing the food from their picnic basket. The mother

86

might have been as much as sixteen, though Theda
doubted it. She wore the same kind of shirt as Ronnie,
her feet were also bare. Her hair was long, and
bleached out, falling straight from the crown of her
head; her skinny brown arms and legs were all elbow
and knee. She ate very little herself, making sure
Ronnie said "thank you" each time a new morsel was
offered.

"You gotta eat too," said the old Aboriginal
woman.

"Me?" grinned Ronnie's mother, "Don't worry bout
me but. I may look like a piece a straw but I've yet to
meet the hurricane could blow me over."

"Do yous know her?" Theda asked one of the
women at her table.

"She was talkin to us at the bus station."

"Baby's father left them by the side of the road
north of Cairns."

"With only a coupla his old shirts to keep the sun
off."

"No money, no food."

"Spect she was seein someone else and he didn't
like it."

"Her own fault, really."

"Yeah, but he shouldn't take it out on the child.
Not her fault her mum's runnin around."
Theda wondered how the kid's mother liked being
talked about and still have to accept the food and
kindness she was offered.

"What she do when he drove off?"

"Caught a lift into town and called her mum."
Theda looked again at the girl's bare, tanned feet, her
straw thatch of hair and broken teeth. Just the sort of
girl that sort of thing would happen to. A tragedy in
waiting. If you were casting for the great Australian
outback movie, you'd pick her to play the rags of the
rags to riches heroine. After that you'd have to change
actresses.

"Want some tea?" asked Theda, "I ordered a pot
and I can't drink it all. I'll ask for an extra cup."
The girl smiled and sat down. Ronnie was asleep on
the coach.

"What's your name? Everyone always talks about you as Ronnie's mum."

"I know. We're sorta celebrities aren't we. Ya always learn kids' names first cause their mums keep yellin at em."

"I'm Theda."

"I'm Billy."

"Billy and Ronnie," smiled Theda, "You make a good couple."

"Know why I called her Ronnie?"

"Tell me."

"After the most powerful man in the world," laughed Billy, "Kid's got to have one thing goin for her."

Theda laughed. "Goin a Perth?"

"Yis. Mum's trine a get me a state housin flat. I'm goin ta ring her tomorrow. See how's it goin."

"Do you get on?"

"No," emphatic. "She's worried about Ronnie, her grandchild and all that."

"I guess so."

"But she sent me money for the bus," Billy added, trying to be fair.

Theda nodded.

"She's angry because Ronnie was born out of wedlock."

Such an extraordinary phrase. Theda'd never heard it said seriously. Straight out of Dolly Parton, like the rest of Billy and Ronnie. Theda shot a quick glance at Billy, but Billy was sipping tea. Maybe she was practising for the social workers.

"I'm crazy about my mum," Theda offered, then decided the best way of finding lesbians is to let them know you're there. "Except that stayin with her means goin into voluntary lesbian exile."

Billy looked up at that. Theda hooked glances with her.

"She live in Perth?" asked Billy.

"Yis."

"Big city. Lotta lesbians there. Ya just have ta look."

"I've been lookin," said Theda.

Billy only shrugged and nodded.

As the bus plunged across the desert, and the heat rose and the sweat dripped, Ronnie and her mother became a common cause for the women passengers. They seemed to identify with a mother's misfortune, even while blaming her for it. They fed Billy and the child, passed orange juice down the bus, offered advice, asked the roadhouse and garage owners along the way if there wasn't an old pair of thongs lying about for the child, a frock or something for the mother. Food, clothes, advice and homilies were all greeted with the same formal gratitude.

When Billy called her mum from Kalgoorlie, and heard she had a flat to move into, the rest of the bus cheered. There was talk of a collection for furniture. It was heart-warming, and after Ranier Theda's heart needed warming, but mopping up men's messes is a way of life for straight women. Theda would have liked it better if they'd done it for love of Billy.

The coach trip was a practice run for Theda's stay in Perth. Robust displays of female kindness: neighbours and relatives popping in to offer help, bringing cakes and jam and vegies, sending husbands to cut the lawn, sons to water the garden and clean the windows. But always that peculiar distance, of lives lived apart, a reticence, reserve. Theda was tempted to ring Ranier long distance just for the intensity of the connection. Why didn't straight women go mad with restraint? They must be the loneliest creatures on earth. At least men don't notice there's anyone else out there. It's amazing what you take for granted while you have your own community around you.

Theda's mother, Olga, was very frail, could not walk more than a few steps, so Theda spent most of her time in the house. Once, when an old friend of Olga's came to spend the day, Theda had gone into town to seek out the café, the pub and the bookshop. She had begun to wonder if straight women's atoms weren't more loosely connected, and lesbian valencies stronger, tighter. If so, her own molecular structure seemed to be slipping, hollow sockets producing a dry crack instead of the usual smooth spring. Perhaps this is what is meant by the phrase "falling apart". As she walked along the street in the brilliant sunshine she searched every female face for a sign, and in every one she saw Ranier. Her despised infatuation seemed now the most lesbian part of her; she had carried Ranier with her from Sydney and that face had not broken up into an assembly of dots but was as solid and resolved as before. As she walked, she felt Ranier beside her; Ranier shared the excitement of finding the location of the café, the disappointment that it had become a gleaming new car rental. Theda had hoped there might still be posters stuck up on the window advertising other events. The car rental was not a lot of use to one whose licence has been suspended. Then it struck her that Ranier did not want to be with her and Theda was left alone on the streets once more. At the bookshop she found lesbian novels to supplement the stock she had brought with her. All books she had read before, and no magic realism, but the sight of the word "lesbian" was a boon, an escape from her mother's kindhearted friends who politely refrained from asking after Theda's husband, boyfriend, sons, knowing these positions to be vacant, not liking to sound the depths of Theda's emptiness. Back at her mother's she rang the pub and discovered there had been a women's night the evening after she arrived; she would have to wait another month.

As the weeks passed, the women's night grew in significance. Theda worried what to wear, how she would get there, whether she had the nerve to go on her own, and what if no one spoke to her when she did get there. She would just have to speak to them. Fill her loneliness with her own effort. She thought about Billy and Ronnie in their new State Housing flat. She wanted lesbians to tell the story to. Her mother had remarked how there were always reports in the papers about rapes by the U.S. Navy up at the flats. Well, she'd said, it's just a lot of women and children living alone so of course the sailors think they're all prostitutes. She said it was understandable. All of human life can be understood, why does comprehension eradicate blame? Why was Billy so certain Theda would find dykes in Perth? Maybe she thought lesbians were like mountain gorgonzola, a specialised taste but available in any large metropolis.

It took a three-hour bus ride with two changes to get to the pub. When Theda spotted the crowd of rowdy dykes queuing to get in, she beamed with the kind of joy she would have radiated if Ranier had said "Come right on over," in response to her epic phone call. After a month away from the smell of lesbians, Theda felt she could put up with almost anything. She was wrong.

"You can't go in there," said a voice.

Theda was about to unload a month's wrath on the owner of the voice when she turned and saw Billy and Ranier with a placard.

"No To Australian Apartheid."

"What's goin on?" demanded Theda, six questions at once.

"They're searchin Aboriginals for knives. If they refuse to be frisked, they can't go in. Whites just pay and enter," said a Black woman with another placard. The promised land receded into a grey horizon.

"Why?" asked a white dyke.

"Manager's orders and the manager's a racist scumbag."

"I've waited a month to get here," said Theda, "Only lesbian thing I could find in the whole of Western Australia." This was no longer the point, even for Theda, but events had so far overtaken her that she clung to the last clear thought she had had, until she could decide how to arrange her emotions.

"If ya wanna meet dykes," said Billy practically, "Ya oughta join the picket."

If intensity had been lacking this last month in Perth, it was crackling here red hot.

"Why didn't you tell me you were a dyke?" Theda demanded, finding Billy an easier target than Ranier. "Especially after I told you."

"I reckoned ya could see for yerself."

"Your smokescreen was pretty thick. Tellin the other women Ronnie's father'd caught you with another man."

"They took one look at me and made it up

themselves. And so did you. 'Poor white trash', as the Americans so sweetly put it."

"I never said that."

"Didn't have ta."

"Yous know each other?" said Ranier.

"I wouldn't say that," said Billy. "Okay, I'm sorry to run you up the garden path, but I didn't reckon those women would look after Ronnie so nice if they knew her mother was a dyke. You'd made up ya mind what a lesbian looked like, and I wasn't it. Go on, admit it."

Theda shrugged.

"Spose you'd like to know what I'm doin in Perth?" said Ranier.

"Oh no," said Theda, "I can make it up all by myself."

CAR SPRAY

[Minnie, London lesbian, is visiting her mother in Australia. Her mother's husband, John, has invited the entire Physics Department of the Uni of W.A. to a dinner party for which he will spend the entire story cooking.]

Minnie   Any of them dykes, Ma?

Beryl   Well, they do say Charles may be gay.

Minnie   Think I'll take the ghost freeway to the beach and watch the sunset.

Beryl   But you're the guest of honour. And there's the doorbell now.

[She answers the door.]

Beryl   Minnie, this is Charles.

Charles   And this is Cinzia.

Cinzia   Call me Chintz.

Beryl   Are you another physicist, Chintz? The room is filling up with physicists.

Charles   No, Chintz is a lawyer, aren't you, Chintz?

Chintz   I'm a lawyer.

Beryl   You must be clever then. I expect you're clever.

Chintz   Charles and I were discussing that in my car on the way up here.

Minnie   What was your verdict?

Charles   No. Not enough room for two brains in one car.

93

Chintz   So you're a writer, Minnie?

Beryl   Oh yes. Let me show you her books. Look, this was the first one with the yellow cover. And this one . . .

Minnie   Ma, I love you, but don't you think it's a bit like showing people my baby photos?

[Beryl kisses Minnie on the top of her head and goes off to have her nice bath in peace. She thinks she might take **Преступление и Наказание**(*Crime and Punishment*) with her, and maybe a large glass of brandy, seeing as the young people are now chatting so nicely together. Much though she admires her daughter's books, Beryl can't help noticing that none of them is 'Crime and Punishment'. Her own, almost irreplaceable, copy of the Russian text has a large brown mark through it from when Beryl sat sunning herself in the garden the time the laundry and the ironing and the cooking and the cleaning all got done on time and there emerged no unforeseen emergency of bloody noses, or premature infants — let us recognise that her daughters are all three over twenty now, and one is eight months pregnant, not Minnie, one hastens to add. Beryl sat in the garden reading her favourite Russian novel in her favourite language with a large magnifying glass because her eyes needed a lot of help these days, when suddenly the page began to smoulder and burn before her and it was not with the repressed passions of Sonja and Raskolnikov but the dear old sun itself. So now, when Beryl can catch a quick quarter hour she usually takes it in the bath.]

[This has been a long diversion from the central, lesbian plot, but Beryl is tired of appearing in her daughter's stories in the role of provider and forehead kisser. She would like it known that she does have a life of her own in which she plans a return to Leningrad where, perhaps, she can make friends with a nice middle-aged Russian lady who will give her an unburned edition of 'C & P' (or '**ПиН**') and maybe some help with those complicated idioms.]

Charles   [reading the cover of the yellow book]

	Sounds like one of those French novels where someone goes somewhere, does something, meets some people and writes about it.
Minnie	Pretty standard plot.
Charles	You know what I mean.
Minnie	That must be most reassuring.
Charles	Short. You know, how French writers specialise in short novels.
Minnie	[nodding] Like Proust, you mean.
Charles	So you work for the same company who publishes you? I thought only the most mediocre writers get published by their friends.
Minnie	I guess Gertrude Stein and Virginia Woolf were pretty mediocre.
Charles	Do you only write for women? Doesn't that cut off a lot of your sales, economically speaking?
Minnie	Statistically speaking there are a few billion people in the world of whom at least 52% are women so, financially speaking, if no man ever read one of my books I'd be laughing.

[The women in the room are all laughing. Minnie hopes she has finished with Charles so she can get back to Chintz. Life among the lesbians has made her forget that men interpret put-downs as come-ons.]

| Charles | So what do you think of Milan Kundera's 'Unbearable Lightness of Being'? |
| Minnie | Charles, let's get one thing clear. I am not going to reply to any question to which the answer is not, and never has been, Anne Bancroft. |

[Charles looks disgruntled and goes off to join the men. They, physicists all, are staring fixedly at Beryl's short wave radio and pondering all possible and potential climactic and other factors which may have caused it to stop receiving Radio Moscow.]

| Chintz | Psst, Minnie, what was the stage name of Anna-Maria Louise Italiano? |
| Minnie | [grinning] Giss a clue. |

Chintz	She starred in 'The Graduate' with Dustin Hoffman.
Minnie	Blimey, this is hard. [Pause] Rita Hayworth?
Chintz	Close. Very close. And that's a good position to be in vis à vis Rita Hayworth.

[Did Chintz really say that, or was it a product of Minnie's fevered brain?]

Chintz	Now, who takes her gloves off in 'Gilda'?
Minnie	Elizabeth Taylor?
Chintz	Nearly. Who starred in 'Who's Afraid of Virginia Woolf'?
Minnie	Lily Tomlin.
Chintz	Very good. Not right, but very good.
Minnie	I was hoping there might be a question about Whoopie Goldberg?
Chintz	Next time. I think you need to be rationed.
Minnie	Okay. Let's get back to you. You're a lawyer . . .
Chintz	An Italian lawyer.
Minnie	Italian?

[For the next twenty minutes Chintz tells Minnie the story of how first her father, and then her mother, and then most of the inhabitants of a little Italian village outside Bari, ended up in Western Australia. As Chintz may well want to tell her story herself, we won't repeat it here. We will, however, say that when Chintz asked Minnie, three days later, how she knew she was a lesbian, Minnie replied: 'You know the old joke about how you know who the dyke is? – She's the one who fronts up to you in the bar, asks you how you are and listens to the answer? Well, when I asked you about yourself you looked me straight in the eyes and answered at length, without giggling, trivialising or letting your eyes wander round the room in search of the real thing. And after that,' Minnie added, 'I just hoped.']

[That was three days later. Let's not anticipate. Chintz is short and has short hair and wears a leather jacket and she is curled up in Minnie's mother's armchair in such a way that Minnie suddenly finds herself imagining she is wrapping her arms around her and kissing her. But Chintz is in Minnie's mother's living room and so cannot be a lesbian even though Minnie, who is also in her mother's living room, is indeed a lesbian. Minnie counts. There are only twenty people in the room and already she and Charles are homosexual so, even if it were not for Minnie's mother's living room, Chintz still could not be a lesbian. Minnie resents the fact that a gay man should have used up half the precious quota.]

[The other women are sitting in corners in their smart jackets while the men discuss inverse sub-semi groups. Beryl signals to Minnie and Minnie and Chintz split up and rescue the women. Chintz leaves early. Minnie wants to run out into the driveway and jump on Chintz' car bonnet and yell Take me hostage but she is much older (ten years) and much taller (two inches) than Chintz (although her hair is much longer) and so, roles, being what they are, it is impossible, it is all quite impossible.]

[Charles, four hours drunker, is declaiming the complexities of his sex life to all and sundry. He is about to start on Chintz' sex life but Beryl is not going to allow it. She has a strong sense of propriety.]

Charles   Chintz has started reading Genet to try and understand me better, Minnie. Do you think she's picked the right author?

Minnie   [who has realised that snubbing Charles only eggs him on] I think the best way to understand anyone is to talk to them.

Charles   But do you think it a useless project for a lesbian to try and understand a gay man?

Minnie   [who wants to say "yes", has just realised a) that Charles has just told her Chintz is a dyke and b) that he is now her only way of contacting the woman] Lesbians have many skills.

[As everyone leaves, Minnie gets Chintz' phone number from Charles.]

Chintz   Like to come to dinner Friday?
Minnie   Love to.

Chintz   I've only just got back from work so we're
         eating out. Indian okay?
[Minnie nods.]

Chintz   Jeeze, it's cold in here.
Minnie   Here. Have my jumper.
Chintz   You came prepared.
Minnie   It's my mother. Won't let me borrow the car
         unless I've a woolly jumper on me. She
         frisks me as I go out the door.
[Chintz kills a cockroach.]
Chintz   Bloody cockroach.
[It takes them an hour and a half to get fed. It takes
them an hour to notice.]
Minnie   So yeah, like I was saying, I'm a radical
         feminist and if you want to call me a
         separatist it won't bother me.
Chintz   I have a confession to make.
Minnie   What? You're a socialist?
Chintz   I don't know what a separatist is.
Minnie   You sure?
Chintz   Well, I just don't understand how they can
         hate men.
Minnie   You sure?
Chintz   Yes. And stop asking if I'm sure. Charles is a
         good friend of mine, I have a lot of time for
         him.
[Minnie thinks maybe she should back off before their
obvious incompatibility drives home.]
Chintz   Anyway, wanna go to a session at the Blue
         Room, Sunday?

Chintz   I'm sorry I'm so late. My mother turned up
         from Albany and made me lasagna.
Minnie   She drove five hundred miles to cook you
         lasagna?
Chintz   She knew I'd be hungry. Three months ago I
         told her I was a lesbian. She told me that
         never would have happened if she hadn't
         come to Australia. She's convinced there are
         no other Italian lesbians. Just her daughter.

Minnie	Course there are. There's Nicole Falda, Karen Liverpool, Betsey Enrico . . .
Chintz	What part of Italy are they from?
Minnie	Brooklyn.
Chintz	I don't think my mother would count that as part of Italy. She was okay, though. I told her I was going to have my car sprayed and I was a bit worried that she'd object because she's very superstitious.

[It's noisy in the pub. Minnie wonders if she heard right.]

Minnie	Why should she object?
Chintz	She's very religious. She might think it was tempting fate, going against the church or something. But she offered to pay for it so in the end me, my mum and my sister all had our cars sprayed.

[Now Minnie knows she heard wrong. She decides to ask strategic questions.]

Minnie	How did it go?
Chintz	Well, mine said there were big changes in the air, a long haired stranger and possible heartache.
Minnie	[laughing] I heard you say you were having your car sprayed not your cards read.

[Chintz laughs hysterically and for the next ten minutes makes up old traditional Italian ceremonies for Minnie where the mother solemnly sprays the dyke daughter's car lavender as a rite of passage. She describes the food, only eaten on that occasion, for which the recipe is carefully guarded and passed from mother to daughter awaiting the birth and driving licence of the dynasty's dykes. However old the daughter is, the ceremony always takes place exactly three months after she has come out to her mother. Chintz' mother's certainty that there are no other Italian dykes in the world must be read as a statement of pride, of the specialness of her daughter and the long time lapse between this car spraying and the last. Minnie suggests, tentatively, that perhaps this Italian custom is simply continuing a much older, more widespread custom dating from the time before cars.]

Chintz   Oh yeah? What did the proud mother do then?

Minnie   Anointed her daughter's hippo with blushful hippo cream.

[And so Minnie explains to Chintz about the hippo cream; the old Egyptian tradition of sparing a hippo's blushes takes on new meaning with the new dyke insights.]

Chintz   Well, I suppose I ought to be going.

Minnie   You in a hurry?

Chintz   Why?

[Awkwardly Minnie leans forward, takes hold of Chintz' chin and kisses her. Chintz moves toward her to ease the angle of the kiss. There are a lot of couples in corners at the Blue Room and they are all kissing and they are all awkward.]

Minnie   Your place or mine? [Is there much point avoiding a cliché when clichés are on your mind?]

Chintz   Not mine. I couldn't cope with passing one of my ex-lovers on my way to the toilet.

Minnie   Not mine. I couldn't subject you to my family's brand of liberalism. I've always had this fantasy of borrowing my mother's camper van, parking in King's Park overlooking the Swan and doing it there.

Chintz   Slumming Australian style? My fantasy is checking into a . . .

Minnie   Sleazy motel?

Chintz   Five star hotel . . .

Minnie   With a swimming pool on the roof?

Chintz   With a swimming pool on the roof and champagne on room service.

Minnie   I don't drink.

Chintz   Don't worry. I'll drink. You swallow.

[They drive to the hotel. Minnie puts coins in the parking meter. Chintz goes into the lobby.]

Minnie   I can't afford this.

Chintz   Don't worry. I'm a lawyer, my services are worth $100 an hour and my firm gets a discount here.

Chintz   You're still worried. We've worried about our clashing politics; we've worried about how young and impressionable I am, and we've worried about the ethics of one night stands. What's left?

Minnie   The parking meter. It'll run out at 8.30 tomorrow morning and my mother will get a parking fine.

Chintz   I would like to say for the record that you are the only dyke in the whole world who connects parking meters with sex.

Minnie   Oh I don't know, some of them "run down Christopher Street caressing the iron breasts of the parking meters."*

Chintz   It is amazing how articulate you remain with someone else's nipple in your mouth.

[pause]

Chintz   Alright. What's the registration?

Minnie   No idea. It's my mother's car.

Chintz   [shaking her head] Hello, Room Service? This is 221. Have someone stick a couple of dollars in the meter of the white Kingswood parked outside the lobby. And if there's more than one Kingswood, fill them all up.

[The day after passes in something of a daze. It felt so easy, so inevitable. Minnie wonders who Chintz is. Sex is a good way to get to know a woman. When you know her already. That night Minnie meets Chintz in a Vietnamese noodle house; either they should be making love, or they should be strangers. Minnie suggests coffee, hoping to prolong the evening until she has pinpointed her anxiety. She drives to an Italian cafe, drops Chintz off and parks. Inside the cafe are all the people from the party, except Beryl who is at her Russian class where Minnie left her earlier in the evening, and John who is, of course, still cooking.]

Charles   Hello you two. Where've you been?

*Fragments From Lesbos, p. 15, Elana Dykewomon, Diaspora Distribution, California, 1981.

[Minnie does not want to join them, but they are
Chintz' friends and this is Chintz' town.]
Minnie   Vietnamese noodle house.
Charles   Which one?
Minnie   It was called the "Hung Long".
[The inevitable jokes are made. They seem to Minnie
to last a long time.]
Chintz   Where've you been?
Charles   To the Da Kow.
[As soon as she hears the name Minnie senses trouble
but feels unable to forestall it. She looks across at
Chintz wondering what her reaction will be. Someone,
not Charles or Chintz or Minnie, makes a joke about
cooking with gas.]
Minnie   [Gabbling] Don't say that. Don't make that
         kind of . . . I hate that kind . . . It's horrible
         . . . It's not funny.
Charles   I think what Minnie's trying to say is that
         kind of joke is cruel and stupid and anti-
         semitic. It trivialises the torture and death of
         six million people.
Someone Well hey, what I say is, if you've got a line,
         use it.
Charles   You don't have a line. You don't have a
         brain cell. You don't have an ounce of . . .
[Minnie has just seen something which makes her feel
sick.]
Minnie   I um, I er have to go now and, um, pick up
         my mother at her Russian class.

Minnie   I wasn't going to pick you up for another
         hour. What happened did the class get cut
         short?
Beryl   No. They went off to a casino with some
         Russian sailors but nice Mrs Katz and I
         didn't want to go. She stayed and helped me
         with my dark ls. Darling, you're driving all
         over the road. Are you alright?
Minnie   Ma, do you know a restaurant called the
         Da Kow?
Beryl   Yes.
Minnie   Well, Charles and them had just eaten there

102

	and they made this horrible joke about the name and then, well, Chintz laughed, at the joke, and I was making love to her last night.
Beryl	Mmm. It's an unfortunate name for a restaurant. People do make jokes about it.
Minnie	People you know?
Beryl	Oh, we had a works dinner there and they made the sort of jokes Charles' friends would make.
Minnie	But what did you do?
Beryl	Observed what sort of people they were and decided not to go out with them again. What more can one do?
Minnie	Tell them what you think.
Beryl	What are you going to do? Ring Chintz up and ask her why she laughed at an anti-semitic joke?
Minnie	Yes of course. That's just what I must do.
Beryl	You lesbians are funny. I can't imagine ringing up a man I'd just slept with and accusing him of anti-semitism when I'm not even Jewish.
Minnie	I can't sleep with someone who could laugh at genocide.
Beryl	I thought you already had. Does sex make you moralistic? Life's rich tapestry: heterosexuals worry about AIDS, lesbians worry about anti-semitism.
Minnie	Chintz, I don't know how to put this so it will sound decorous but just now, at the cafe, that friend of Charles made that joke about the Da Kow . . .
Chintz	I know. It was stupid. But Charles shut him up.
Minnie	But you, I thought you, I mean you laughed, didn't you?

[Minnie knows Chintz laughed. She saw her. She was watching her the whole time. Minnie prays that Chintz will not simply deny it now that she hears Minnie is upset.]

Chintz	I didn't laugh at that joke.

[Minnie feels sick.]

Chintz   I was feeling very nervous.

Minnie   Why?

Chintz   All evening, like you were testing me; did I measure up to your high standards. Then when we walked into the cafe, I could feel everyone tense up. No. When I came in, it was fine. Then they saw I was with you and there was this tension.

Minnie   Why? Because they had to recognise us as lesbians?

Chintz   They already know perfectly well that I'm a dyke.

Minnie   Then why?

Chintz   Because you were so short with Charles at the party. They thought you'd try to put them down.

Minnie   How do you know?

Chintz   I don't know. I just sensed it.

Minnie   They didn't have to make anti-semitic jokes because I made them uneasy. [And you didn't have to laugh at them, Minnie thinks but does not say.]

Chintz   Some of them are creeps, agreed. Have you rung me up in the middle of the night to accuse me of anti-semitism? Aren't you meant to be sending me roses or do you feminist dykes do everything different? I wasn't laughing. My face was smiling nervously. I'd been smiling nervously all evening only you didn't notice.

Minnie   I'm sorry. I'm glad. Thank you for explaining. Did you get home alright?

Chintz   Yes. Charles gave me a lift.

Minnie   Bully for big buddy Charles. You know I put him down at the party because he walked in the door declaring you were stupider than him.

Chintz   My noble protectrix. That was just one of Charles' jokes. He was being ironic.

Minnie   You didn't mind at the time. After you left, dear old Charlie was dead set on telling the world all about your sex life.

Chintz   So you rang me in the middle of the night to
         chat about Charles? I mentioned this before
         but you didn't take the hint, I am not going
         to reply to any question which is not, and
         never has been, accompanied by half a dozen
         red roses.

[Chintz hangs up.]

SACCHARIN CYANIDE

Lauren was just reflecting that she wouldn't want a car if someone were to ring up and offer her one, when the phone rang. Last time the phone had rung, three days ago, it was someone from a timeshare company in Spain offering her a free television. There is no such thing as a free television. There is always the licence fee and, for this set, you had to sit through a two hour presentation in Leicester Square on the glories of collective tenancy. The penultimate time the phone had rung, sometime last week, it was a young woman offering a free quote on a new fitted kitchen.

"I don't have a kitchen," said Lauren.

When they rang offering free insurance quotes, free help with buying your council house and a free questionnaire, Lauren would reply,

"Oh my, how exciting. I am glad you've rung. Now just wait while I get a pen."

She would put the receiver back on its cradle a couple of days later. Often the sales negotiator would still be extolling the finer aspects of the insurance cover, plastic waste disposal, political party . . .

Lauren answered the phone. It was her brother. Would she like his old car. Free.

"There is no such thing as a free car," she replied. "There's the M.O.T. . . ."

"It's got eleven months run."

"The insurance . . ."

"Included in my cover."

"Licence . . ."

"Bought my annual last month."

"Then why're you giving it to me?"

"I just won a metallic blue Ford Grenada with air conditioning, fuel injection and six year anti-corrosion guarantee."

"What do you have to do for that?"

"Shake hands with a household name and collect the keys."

"Aren't they going to pull down your existing kitchen, reinsure you for twice your market value or make you vote Conservative?"

"Got the kitchen done in January on the last insurance deal and I've voted Conservative ever since they sold me my council house."

Despite her better judgement, Lauren shook her brother's hand, collected the keys and drove off in a five year old beige Ford Fiesta. It was the ideal car for gliding through road blocks; the cops would never be able to distinguish it from all the other beige Ford Fiestas they had already searched. Not that road blocks figured high on Lauren's horizon. She was at that moment reflecting that a car would be useful for fetching calor gas refills and she'd be able to park at the new Sainsbury's to take advantage of their economy 36 pack of Andrex which she'd never been able to carry home before.

As Lauren kicked open her flat door, arms laden with a harvest festival of toilet rolls, gas cannister waiting at the bottom of the stairs, the phone rang. Assuming it would be aluminium double glazing or timeshare parking, Lauren picked up the receiver. It was Muriel from the Women's Centre. Since Lauren now had her own transport, would she mind collecting the hi-fi system for tonight's disco?

"How . . . ?"Lauren began.

"Delia saw you in the parking lot up at Sainsbury's. She couldn't help noticing you walked round to the driver's side."

The phone had used up a fortnight's calls in one

day. Lauren unplugged it. The next four hours she spent transcribing tapes and recording the contents of various official letters for her boss, a blind research doctor. Then she set off to collect the hi-fi equipment. The car wouldn't start.

"Battery," she thought. And, scraping together what car folklore she could remember, "Choke."
She had passed her test at the first attempt a month ago, but she'd never had to start a cold car. It came to her door warm from the last pupil.

Lauren drove neatly off and into the main road. Then she stalled. She stalled again at the zebra crossing, at the traffic lights and in a queue of traffic waiting to turn right. She stalled five times in the first mile, the last time right in front of a police car with its siren screaming. After that she turned into a side street, stopped, considered the situation and formally burst into tears. She slammed the door and strode off up the road, turning her back on the car never to return. She was half way up the street when it struck her that if she left the car in the middle of the road the police would be knocking at her door. She had closed the choke and reversed into a more orthodox parking position, when she remembered that a hundred women were depending on her to add grace and rhythm to their finger clicking, hip swaying, heel tapping, low diving, slow jiving courtships. By now the engine was purring prettily. She reached the Women's Centre only twenty minutes late. Muriel was on the front step.

"At last. Any later and you'd have been as popular around here as Edwina Bacon."
Edwina Bacon was the local word for poison.

The disco was blasting, fingers, hips and heels moving to a well-regulated beat.

"Okay Muriel," said Lauren, "So tell me about Edwina Bacon. If you old ones don't pass on the gossip, us youth of today might make a mistake and invite her back onto the collective."

"Over my dead body."

"Funny how everyone offers their corpse whenever Edwina's mentioned."

"That woman is poison. She's a power mad, puritanical racist tyrant. Took a full-blown court case to get her out of here. Even then she carted half the stuff away with her."

"What stuff?"

"Books, magazines. I don't know, nothing valuable. Don't suppose she even wanted them. Just a sour loser, had to grab something."

"What was the row about?"

"Row? That woman created so many rows you couldn't get to the bottom of one of them. But the big thing was the café. She was determined to get that café closed down, called in an outside auditor, said someone was fiddling the books. Paranoia. The others were running the café very well without her and making a handsome profit, so Edwina had to find something against it. And there were the film nights. They organised a series of lesbian movies in the café. Edwina picked on one and declared it soft porn."

"Was it?"

"That wasn't the point. Edwina had never seen it. It was for her like a successful film series was the last straw in losing control of the Centre."

"I don't get it," said Lauren.

"There's a lot about Edwina nobody gets," said Delia, popping into the office to pick up some raffle tickets. "She said the lesbian film was porn but in the court settlement she opted to take all the 'violence against women' stuff in the Centre. There was a whole section: books, films, tapes . . ."

"Oh yes, that's right," said Muriel. "I forgot. Edwina had collected most of it, so I suppose it was fair."

"And amongst that stuff was the film she'd made all the fuss about. Can you beat it?"

"Sounds like she was confiscating it," observed Lauren.

"I heard she turned her spare room into her very own porn library," said Muriel.

"That woman's sicker than saccharin cyanide," said Delia.

"There is no saccharin to Edwina," Muriel corrected.

"Let's dance. I'm sick of Edwina Bacon. All that was over with five years ago but it's still the big scandal," said Delia.

"Once you hear of Edwina, you never hear the last of her," said Muriel. "That woman is . . ."

"I know," said Lauren, "Poison."

"Paraquat," confirmed Muriel.

"Harpic," added Delia.

"Neat lye," was Lauren's suggestion.

The merry list was interrupted by Joy.

"These women just told us that some boys have been smashing car windows in the street. Any of you parked out there?"

"Couldn't be my car," said Lauren, "After all the trouble I had getting here, that would be too much bad luck."

"Better go to the cop shop," advised Muriel, shaking her head over the broken glass. "You'll need a crime number for the insurance. I don't know why they do it, unimaginative vandals. Smashed car windows wouldn't make me happy."

"Don't start. Give them imagination, they'll smash an atom," said Lauren.

The glass was everywhere: all over the seats, the floor, in the glove compartment. There were even some fragments on top of the sun shades.

"Offside front," noted the policeman, "Park it with the broken window to the road, less risk of opportunist crime. And don't leave any valuables in it." Lauren decided to leave the car outside the station over night, safe there as anywhere. Nothing in it but cassettes she'd been transcribing and no one in their right mind would bother to filch those. In the morning she rang her brother.

"I see," he said abruptly, "Where is it now?"

"Outside Wood Green Police Station," said Lauren.

She did not want this gift car used to apprise her brother of her every move.

"Which garage are you taking it to?"

"Dunno. Nearest. Why?"

"Insurance."

"Nonsense. Muriel told me that was automatic. Wouldn't even affect the no-claims bonus."

"How'd she know? Just tell me which garage and have them send the bill to me."

Lauren shrugged into the phone, leafed through the *Yellow Pages* and read out the name of a garage up the road. As good as any, no doubt.

What happened next, and in what order, would have slipped Lauren's mind, like washing hung out to dry in other people's gardens, were she not soon to have reason to go over every fine detail. She dropped the car off at the garage as arranged. Then she walked home, about five minutes away. That evening, just as she was pouring a second cup of tea, she remembered that the tapes were still in the car and she needed to finish indexing them. This was the most skilled part of the job: without a proper index Dr Akoba would have to listen through fifteen cassettes before she could find the part of research she wanted to quote. Lauren composed the initial index, being most familiar with Dr Akoba's work; then she gave it to the RNIB braille pool who would translate the aural into the tactile form. Reconstructing these details was easy because all braille work was sent off at the end of the month and this was the 29th, so even if she hadn't remembered, Lauren could have guessed quite accurately that she would be finishing off index work that evening.

She put a saucer on top of her cooling tea, shrugged back into her coat, and walked round the corner to the garage. The yard was dark and Lauren had not thought, not being in the country, to bring a torch. She located her car and began gathering up cassettes. She could find only fourteen in the glove compartment where she'd left them. Maybe one had fallen on the floor when she was clearing up the glass. She searched under the seats, hard work in the dark.

111

Finally she bent right over and began to feel around with her fingers, worried she might collect an inadvertent splinter. And there was the missing cassette, or rather the missing cassettes, for her finger tips felt the hard plastic of two cases. She dropped them into her coat pocket. Did she glimpse a shadowy figure approaching the garage as she left? Or did hindsight provide the figure after the fact? Lauren hurried home.

She began to check references to 'sickling', certain she'd missed one on tape thirteen. She listened carefully right the way through, still the reference eluded her. Maybe at the beginning of tape fourteen? What a waste of time; which just showed the importance of a trustworthy index. She surveyed the stack of tapes. One of them was unmarked; she didn't remember putting any blank cassettes in the car. More likely she just hadn't written its series number on the J card. Better have a quick listen and mark it up now.

But the unmarked cassette was indeed blank. She fast forwarded a little to make sure. Nothing. Then, as she poured milk into yet another cup of tea, she heard a little click. And a woman's voice, not her own. The voice of an old woman, calling for help. Screaming. Oh my God, screaming blue murder in a shrill, breaking pitch. Then the woman spoke,

"Help me, please, help. Are you there? Can you hear me? Police! He's in the house, he broke in. He's coming up the stairs. I can hear him. Please." Then a muffled noise, a thud, but the voice went on, now an inarticulate gurgling, choking, gasps. Then nothing. As though a phone had been shoved back in its cradle.

Lauren let the tape play right through to the end, until the transcriber clicked. She was unable to move, to think, to breathe. She was terrified. Terror was the man who had broken in, who was, even now, climbing the stairs towards her flat, who would open the door and swoop down upon her, wrap his hands around her throat and choke the life from her. Her body was old, it could not move fast, she had little strength in her arms and she walked heavily with the aid of a stick. She could not get away; there was nowhere to hide. She had rung the police knowing they would be too late but unable to give up and go, abandon hope. Her screams were pleas for something to intervene, for a residual goodness in the air she had been breathing for eighty three years, for general indignation that the world was so brutal a place for old women, to come forward now and throw her attacker down the stairs.

At last Lauren roused herself, switched the machine off and sank into an armchair. She was shaking. A bath, perhaps, a warm bath and all the mindless small actions needed to accomplish it. Surrounded by hot water and many soap suds, Lauren thought over what had happened and what she should do. Clearly she had picked up a tape which did not belong to her. How it had got into her car, and when, she had no idea. But these were rational thoughts, devised to block out others. Who was that old woman? What had happened to her? Had she been choked to death by an intruder while in the very act of calling the police for help? Or, was it part of a play, a radio play, perhaps? Lauren wondered. Had she inadvertently recorded a few frightening moments from a play? Or, from the News? There was that woman, what was her name: Syriol Lewis? She had indeed been murdered in just that way. Lauren sought desperately to remember. It had been on the News earlier that month. That must be it. She must have had a blank in the recorder and turned on the radio at the same time. Lauren began to feel a little less shaky. She played with the soap suds, heaping them up into piles and calling them sheep as she had when she bathed with her brother years ago. It was a long excerpt for radio news, though, two minutes at least. Very long. And so frightening, surely there must have been complaints if even Lauren, who was used to listening to unpleasant recordings through her job, had been terrified. Lauren surveyed her store of bath oils, bath pearls, bath essence, bath salts and bath seeds. She threw a mixture into the water and turned the hot back on to produce a churning Hellespont of foam. She smelt like Sissinghurst on a hot day when all the sap is rising and a thick cloud of perfume hovers over the flowerbeds. Simple comfort to calm her until she was recovered enough to think again. Before she took her hot water bottle and warm milk to bed, Lauren threw the poison cassette into the dustbin. The smell of all the bath scents wafted around her as she raised the bin lid: sweet and rotten. Saccharin cyanide.

Next day passed in a leaden whirl. Lauren had to rush through the rest of the index without checking back over earlier work. Dr Akoba was as pleasant and courteous as always but clearly impatient. Lauren was a conscientious worker, and, knowing the index was not up to her usual scratch, she phoned the braillers and explained that they might have to pay closer attention than usual to make sure everything tied up. Dr Akoba had overheard the phone call and told Lauren off. It simply was not the braillers' job to check the work of the indexer. Did Lauren need more time? Why didn't she deliver the new tapes to the RNIB herself later next week; now that she had her own car it shouldn't be too much trouble. A reasonable solution, but Lauren was in no mood for polite reason. She would very much have liked to confide in the Doctor about the poison cassette but after she'd been ticked off it hardly seemed appropriate.

That evening she had a phone call from the garage. The owner didn't know how to put it; did she want the good news or the bad news first?

"The good news. I've had such bad luck with that car I could do with some good news."

"Well, we've fixed the side window for you. Won't even lose your no-claims bonus," said the owner.

"And the bad?"

"It's been in an accident and, I'm afraid, it's a write-off."

"You're joking. Look, just don't. It's too much. I'm sorry, but I can't take a joke at the moment. I really can't."

"No. It's true. Another car bashed into it. A volvo. Built like a tank, volvo, built like a tank."

"Was anyone hurt?" asked Lauren weakly.

"Fortunately not. And we've got an independent witness so it'll come out of the volvo's insurance."

"I don't believe it," said Lauren, "I don't believe it. It can't be a write-off. I've only just got it."

"Want to dispute with their insurers?" asked the garage owner. "You could do; we'd back you. We feel a little bit guilty cause one of our mechanics was driving it at the time."

They ought to feel more than a little bit guilty: it was their fault. What the hell had the car been doing out on the road anyway; weren't they just fixing the window?

"We had to take it round the block once we'd finished it," said the garage owner, as if answering Lauren's unspoken question. "Not enough room in the yard to keep them there when they're fixed."

Lauren rang her brother.

"Oh bad luck," he said with the Raj drawl he was cultivating now he owned his own council house. "Better still, I have a very good chap in south London who could fix it for you much quicker. Used to weld World War Two bombers. Very good chap. Tell your garage they're off the case and my man will tow the car tomorrow morning."

Lauren felt, if anything, relieved that the car was going back where it came from. It had brought her nothing but suffering. She would go to the RNIB by bus and forget she'd ever had a car. Right now she really must get on with checking the index.

Lauren looked forward to a calming few hours with no interruptions. When there was time to do it properly, she enjoyed the precision and system of her work. She went to the shelves which held her copies of the latest 'Sickle Cell' tapes. She had left them in number order last night, but now they were all out of sequence. It didn't make sense. Someone trying to steal Dr Akoba's sickle cell secrets? Marvellous, let them develop a cure! What was happening? Someone must have broken in, gone through the tapes and not known how to put them back in order, or even, perhaps, that there was any order. They were very clearly numbered, for anyone who read braille. A sudden suspicion occurred to Lauren and she darted into the kitchen. Under a pile of wet tea leaves lay the poison cassette she had thrown away the night before.

It ought all to fall into place: her brother's second hand car, the broken window, the accident, the poison cassette and the break-in. For the life of her, Lauren could not make sense of any of it. What had it to do with the death of Syriol Lewis? for Lauren was uncomfortably certain that it was the murdered woman who connected the sharp fragments. All day Lauren had tried to get on with her work and be sensible, and all day the old woman's dying screams had echoed in her head. She had to do something.

The phone rang.

"Hullo, my dear. I hope I'm not disturbing you," said a familiar voice.

"Oh no," said Lauren, "I'm glad you rang."

"I was a bit short with you today and you know the old saying, 'Let not the sun set on your displeasure', so I want to say I'm sorry if I was harsh."

"Dr Akoba, that's very kind of you. But it was true, it is my job to do the index, not the braillers'."

"Is everything all right at home?"

"Yes, only . . ."

"Only?"

Lauren told the Doctor about finding the cassette.

"Very nasty. Sounds like the Moors murderers recording those poor children's cries," was Dr Akoba's first comment. She did not appear to think it could be a simple practical joke.

"What would anyone do with such a recording?"

"I don't know much about it, but there's a whole market in 'snuff tapes' as they call them. I tell you who would know, the young woman at the Bacon Library. She was very helpful when I was collecting information on female genital mutilation. But I think you should take that tape straight down to the police station. You don't know what you may be dealing with."

Dr Akoba rarely recommended the police station.

Lauren pondered in silence. The police already had a copy of the tape, or it would not have been

116

mentioned on the radio. They weren't exactly known for their efforts to stamp out violence against women. Besides, and an even nastier idea occurred to her, the car had sat outside Wood Green cop shop all night with a broken window, ideal for some bent copper to hide his latest money-spinner. Maybe she should find out more about these 'snuff tapes'. If she could stomach it. She looked up the Bacon Library in the phone book.

"The Bacon Library is closed now. Opening hours are from ten a. m. to six p.m. Tuesdays and from nine a.m. to one p.m. Saturdays. Researchers from abroad on short stays may arrange an appointment outside these hours. If you wish to lodge material, or have any other message, please leave your name . . ."

"This is Lauren de Haan and I, well, I wanted information really. Someone said, that is, Dr Akoba told me, well, I need to know more about 'snuff tapes'. Oh, and I think I'd like to lodge some material."
As she made the offer it occurred to Lauren that a library might indeed be a good place for the poison cassette.

Hardly had she put the phone down, but it rang again.

"Bacon Library. Lauren de Haan, please."
It was one of those abrasive English school mistress voices which will always make sure to pronounce the girl's name right even while delivering the soundest tongue-lashing.

"Yes? Er, speaking."

"You want to lodge some material."

"Well, yes and . . ."

"You are not a member."

"No. I'm afraid not. Is it members only?"

"You wish to apply for membership."

"I suppose I should. Do I just fill in a form?"

"You must state the nature of your research and pay a joining fee."

Sunday found Lauren in Broxby-After-Bliss knocking at the door of the Bacon Library. A tall thin woman showed her in.

117

"I am Edwina Bacon," the woman said.

Silence.

"I see," said Edwina at last, "You have heard of me."

Lauren shrugged. "All that was five years ago. Things change."

"They do not," said Edwina. "I was right then, and I'm right now. If I hadn't been right you would not now be seeking information in my library, Europe's largest collection on violence against women. If I had been right quicker, you would have been able to consult my material in the comfort of your local Women's Centre."

Edwina's tone went straight to Lauren's backbone, rubbed sandpaper in between her vertebrae, pinching nerves as it went.

"You want to know about snuff tapes," Edwina informed her.

Lauren nodded.

Edwina showed her rooms filled with magazines, rooms filled with videos, rooms with tapes, books, letters; a catalogue of horrors, an anatomy of the female body sliced thin, sliced into specialised sections for specialised atrocities; from the new born baby to the old, old woman, the myriad uses and abuses to which flesh of different elasticity could be put.

"So much?" said Lauren.

"The way violence against old women is going," Edwina said, "I'll have to build another alcove."

"You're cynical," said Lauren, "I didn't expect that."

Edwina looked at her. "I wouldn't have thought anything would surprise you about Edwina Bacon."

"I don't know you."

"No one does."

That old line. No one knows me. No one understands me. What was Lauren doing here? Peering into the dusty corners of Women's Liberation Movement history? More like raking through the accumulated hairs and slime and tea leaves of a partially blocked drain.

"Why don't you tell me what you're here for?" Edwina suggested. "Cut short this agony."

Agony.

"Is it that bad?"

"You can hardly expect me to be pleased to see you," said Edwina.

"I don't know you," Lauren repeated.

"No," said Edwina, "You don't. But you know what you've heard."

"I heard you were asked to leave the Women's Centre. That they had to take you to court. You were . . . very . . . suspicious, and the others couldn't work with you," said Lauren, "Something about having the café investigated and objecting to a film night."

"'Suspicious'," savoured Edwina, "Is that what they say these days? The movement has grown . . . polite. I thought I was poison. Saccharin cyanide."

"Well, what did happen?" asked Lauren.

"You're opening old wounds."

"I seem to have opened them by walking in here. Has no-one else from the Centre ever been to the Bacon Library?"

"They haven't the wit. They want to have fun. They want to have a nice day. An endless series of endlessly nice nice days. They want to include every woman who ever lived in their all-inclusive 'we' but they don't want to think about the violence men do which binds us, binds us to each other, binds us hand and foot. Or the women who help the men and do their binding."

"I would find it hard to live in a place like this," Lauren gestured at the walls lined with card indexes in case of computer break-down, "In the midst of all this horror."

"We all live in the midst of it," retorted Edwina, but more softly now, as though the constant abrading of her sandpaper voice was wearing itself down into the finer sand of an ocean beach. "And we all find it hard. I prefer to know; in all circumstances, I prefer to know. I cannot say with those others, 'I can't bear to look', 'don't tell me, it's too upsetting'."

Edwina's body was as taut and as finely balanced as a

119

bicycle wheel, the spokes sprung out from the centre with the grace of the lightest of the new alloys, but the balance was so fine, each spoke tuned so high, that any dart or arrow coming horizontally, when the whole, meticulous make-up of the body was toward the road ahead in one, unwavering line, must throw her over, spokes snapping against the one pressure they could not, for their own nature, guard against.

"Do not mistake me for a spider's web," said Edwina, with a hint, almost, of amusement in her eye, "I am thin but not frail."

"I have heard what the women at the Centre say of you," said Lauren, "I would like to know your story."

"My story?" Edwina paused, then let it pass. "I was prosecuted by my friends. I lost the Centre I built. I was publicly vilified. Women spat at me, or they crossed the street to avoid me."

"Why?"

"'Political Differences'. I was, even then, the national expert on violence against women. I see you bridle at the word 'expert', a well-trained response, but we are not horses. We were all supposed to be 'equal', weren't we? But I knew what was going on, and those women did not. They could have known, but they didn't want to. The woman running the café was an agent."

Agents. Oh brother. And what a sense of bathos.

"I checked the accounts. There was too much coming in. Regular payments from an unlisted source. How do you prove that? I notice, however, that they never opened the café again. Just couldn't quite manage, somehow, to balance the books."

"I heard there was a film . . ." said Lauren.

"Pornography. Lesbian pornography," said Edwina. "Why the hell should I spend every moment of my waking life for years and years and years setting up a Centre for women, a place for lesbians to feel comfortable and have a good time together, oh yes, I wanted a nice day too, collecting massive evidence of the profits and networks of the money men make on buying and selling horrors done to our female bodies, only to have two lesbians make the same kind of film and show it at my Centre? It is not different when lesbians do it, it is merely worse. Merely worse."

It had been a long time since Lauren had heard anything approaching a political opinion, let alone a passionately held political opinion. It happened to be a different opinion from her own, but she felt a grudging respect for a woman who could maintain her passion for so many years with no-one to say "how right you are."

"You are looking at me as though I was crazy," Edwina observed drily.

"Oh no," said Lauren, "I feel a, a . . . a grudging respect for you."

"Why do you grudge me respect? You have come here to my library because you think I'm the only one who can help you. Do you grudge my help? The circumstances which have put me in a position to help you?"

Lauren sighed. It gave her time to think. She remembered this. This prickly, on your toes way of talking, where what you said mattered because the other woman was listening, acutely, to the phrasing, and the tone, every nuance. And Edwina had kept this method alive over five years, by herself?

"Why don't I make us a cup of coffee," Edwina was saying. "Then you can tell me what you're looking for, and need so much that you're prepared to venture into my lair to seek it. Rage is tiring and, probably, misdirected."

Lauren smiled, a little smile to herself it was meant to be, but then she laughed. Edwina looked down upon her, consideringly. It would have been too hard for her to smile, now, after so many years of stiff-lipped, straight-backed silence. Her mouth wouldn't do it, couldn't find the grooves. She cast around for something else.

"There's cream," she said at last. "One of the researchers brought strawberries and cream. Would you like cream in your coffee?"

Edwina listened while Lauren retold the story of the cassette and Syriol Lewis. By the end Lauren found herself shaking. It had been hard to keep going all week with that piteous voice ringing in her ears. The shaking embarrassed her. She was afraid she would cry.

"The Lewis tape," Edwina was saying, "I thought that would surface sooner or later."

"What?" said Lauren.

"As soon as I heard it on the radio," said Edwina, "I knew what it was."

"What?" said Lauren again.

"Well, you were right. It's a snuff tape. They had it played on the air for authentication."

Lauren could not follow. She had hoped for reassurance, she was not getting it.

"To raise the value," said Edwina.

Lauren frowned, then shook her head.

"There is a lot of money in turkey porn these days. Sex with old women."

"Stop. You're making me feel sick."

"I think Syriol Lewis must have felt a lot worse."

"You mean, someone murdered her, recorded what they did, and sent that recording to the police?"

"Possibly someone on the police force. So they could be sure to get the story onto the news."

"And some man listens to it and jerks off?"

"Probably. But what they'll do is edit that voice and those screams into a porn movie – real terror, as seen on TV. Or, in this case, as heard on BBC Radio News."

Lauren stared at the tape, still in her hand. Sick. Sick. Sick.

"It isn't true," she said.

Edwina only looked at her. "Have some more coffee."

"What can we do?" asked Lauren, unaware in the fear of the moment that she had included Edwina in the solution.

"I think you should be careful," replied Edwina. "They won't like to think a copy of their tape has gone astray."

"You mean I'll get back to find my flat turned upside down, drawers on the floor, dustbin emptied on the carpet?"

"It depends whether that's the master or a copy," said Edwina. "If you're lucky, it's only a copy. Tell me again how the tape turned up, when, how you got the car, everything."

So Lauren told her everything.

"Your brother was very keen to trace your movements," said Edwina at last.

"For the insurance," said Lauren. "He needed to know because the car was still on his insurance."

"Convenient."

Lauren said nothing.

"I think," said Edwina, slowly, "You should make another copy of the tape, take this one to the police and phone your brother. Tell him all about it; it was frightening finding it and you just don't want the car back. Girls are superstitious about these things. He'll know that."

"I don't see . . ."

"Whoever put that tape in your brother's car will be very anxious to get it back. They will, by now, have gone through your flat inch by inch. It would, in a way, be better if your brother was involved in it because he can call off his watch dogs."

"My brother? My brother has nothing to do with it. You're letting your imagination run away with you. My brother is not like that. He just happened to let me have his old car," said Lauren, as evenly as she could. Edwina was trying to scare her, use fear to win her over. Well, she'd made a mistake throwing Lauren's brother into the plot. That was plain ridiculous. Not to say insulting.

"Your brother rings up out of the blue to offer you a car. A car you never even suggested you might want. He says he's won a new one in some competition. Next day you phone and tell him the car's in the garage getting a window fixed. He makes a big performance how he needs to know which garage. That night you find the snuff tape. Next day your whole tape collection has been tampered with. Then some volvo writes off your car and your brother has it towed back to south London. Lauren, that guy's in it up to his neck, and trying to use you to throw someone off the trail."

"Stop this, Edwina. Stop it at once. You're not going to intimidate me like some little student or a new acolyte. The whole story is fantastic, it's a complete perversion of what happened."

"Then where did the tape come from?"

"I don't know. Someone put it in my car by mistake."

"Like leaving an umbrella on a bus? I suppose that man's hands around Syriol Lewis' neck were a mistake too."

"What man? Edwina? Are you saying? Christ that's sick, that is perverted. You're crazy, you're . . ."

"Poison?" supplied Edwina. "That's where all our careful analyses always fall down. We never can believe, really believe, that it could be our own brothers, our little brothers, our gay brothers, our Black brothers, our Jewish brothers, our poor, oppressed, working class brothers. Well, it's your choice: believe me and follow through or back off; tell the world you met Edwina Bacon and she's as poisonous as ever. Then convince yourself it's my mind, not your world."

ANGEL ALICE

"I'll be the only cape-coloured queer there," said Gaylord.

"And I'll be the only fourteen year old fag hag," said Angel.

It was quite a party.

"What does your friend drink, dear?" asked Shindy, Angel's mother, as she put the glasses onto trays.

"Dry sherry," said Angel, "And I drink Guinness."

"Indeed," said Shindy.

"If she practises all the adult vices now, whatever will she do when she's older?" expostulated Lemuel, Angel's father, hands full of corks and bottle tops.

"Perfect them," shrugged Shindy.

"Probably be a teetotal Tory spinster living in a bedsit in Streatham," said Angel cheerfully.

"With delirium tremens and a bad dose of clap," finished Hillary, Angel's little brother.

Shindy sighed.

Angel met Gaylord at a drama class in the East End.

"Why do you get all the best parts?" she had greeted him, "Reverse discrimination?"

Gaylord had laughed. "Not at all. Donald fancies me."

"Didn't know Donald was bent."

"He's not. Just a nice normal homo like the rest of us."

"Count me out," said Angel.

"What a waste," said Gaylord.

"I'm perfectly well-adjusted, thank you," retorted Angel.

"But think what you're missing."

"I'd miss you either way."

Gaylord laughed again. He and Angel improvised a relationship in which Angel made him laugh, frequently, and without quite understanding what was funny. For his part Gaylord provided the perfect escort: old enough and male enough for Shindy to allow her daughter out with him, but safe enough and fascinating enough for Angel to want to go. Over the next two years they went to all the gay pubs and clubs of which Gaylord or his friends were members.

"Hello," said a falsetto, "Fleet's in."

Gaylord was wearing a starched white sailor suit, perfect setting for his cafe con leche complexion.

"And he's brought Alice with him, bless her little cotton socks."

Angel looked nearer twelve than sixteen with her thick blonde hair, but no bouncer was to bounce her for another decade. Not till she returned freshly-dyked with a crew cut and Doc Marten boots did they take her for a young boy and throw her out. For the moment at least, she looked like a class drag act.

"To Alice and the Sailor," toasted a hefty barman with a Gary Glitter scowl.

"A dry sherry for me and a pint of Guinness for my friend," Gaylord ordered as Angel looked round at some of the most beautiful men she had seen in her life. All so clean, so young slim tall angular, and they all wore yellow V neck sweaters.

126

"Likes it foamy, does she?" jeered the barman.

"Don't cram your mind with useless data," replied Gaylord, "The lady doesn't know you exist."

The barman pointed to the Guinness. "You should be drinking that. Black, bitter, cold and thick."

"You were a cliché before you were born," said Gaylord, picking up the drinks and turning away. But the barman could not leave it alone.

"Does she fuck?" he asked in urgent Anglo-Saxon monosyllables.

"Why don't you ask her?" said Gaylord.

"I'm talking to you."

"I gave up boorish louts with their brains in their buttocks," said Gaylord. "Why don't you go vandalise a phone box?" He joined Angel in the far corner with a splendid view of the pool table.

"Did he want to put you in a play too?" asked Angel.

"He did," said Gaylord. "But I didn't like the dialogue."

"So," said Gaylord, "Why did you leave Africa?"

"My mother wanted to go," said Angel. "She said there wasn't anywhere in Africa that white people didn't benefit from the oppression of blacks."

"There isn't anywhere in the world that white people don't benefit from the oppression of blacks. That's what South Africa has done for you, and to you, and against you. It's the scapegoat for all your dreams of unearned promotion," said Gaylord. "My white friends with their careful consciences switch the television off when a South African comes on. They do not switch off for a white Australian."

"But that's different," said Angel. "Individual acts, not state edicts."

"I could give you facts and figures," said Gaylord, "But then you would just have to add Australia to the list of places nice white people must boycott."

"You were thinking of something more radical?" said Angel with enthusiasm.

"I'm not much interested in politics," said Gaylord.

"Personally I'd rather forget I was born the only black son of a white South African family. I want to be elegant, cultured, sophisticated. . ."

Angel glanced at Gaylord's beautifully manicured finger nails.

". . . and just a little bit camp," Gaylord laughed at himself. "Growing up in the Mission in Swaziland, visiting my mother at night by walking over the mountains, fleeing to London at the first opportunity, is sophisticated only with a certain determinedly limited perspective. I offered my services to the liberation struggle but they seemed more concerned with my homosexuality."

"I suppose you epitomised Western decadence," grimaced Angel.

"And there was me thinking I'd made it all up by myself," laughed Gaylord.

"Surely breaking up couples because of their sex is as bad as breaking up families because of their race. What are they going to do? Institute pass laws for homosexuals?"

"At the moment your naivety's charming, Alice," replied Gaylord, "But don't rely on it as your only social coin. You'll find it won't age well."

"Angel," said Shindy, as her daughter dropped bottles of Liquid Gumption into the shopping trolley, "It's wrong to call him Gaylord."

"We've been quarreling about this for two years," said Angel, "Why don't you give it up, Mum? English people can't pronounce Xolile."

"We could say 'Golleelay'," suggested Shindy, "An approximation."

"Why not call him John like the missionaries did? A nice English name. Is it impossible to call him what he wants to be called?"

"Does he realise?"

"Of course he realises."

"You two see a lot of each other."

"Yes, Mum. We talk, you know. We got a lot to say."

"Where do you go?"

"Gay bars mostly."

"Why?"

"That's where our friends are. Gaylord'd get slaughtered in a straight pub."

"Are you sure they're your friends?"

"Mum, they're nice. Melvin taught me to play pool and Rodney always dances with me. They don't just leave me in a corner with my pint of Guinness."

"How can you drink that stuff?"

"Oh, it's just for show, me and Gaylord swop back and I sip his sherry."

"For heaven's sake," said Shindy, once they'd finally emerged on the street, "How grubby. You huddle in the dark toying with overpriced drinks, dancing with gay men who are eyeing each other up over your shoulder, saying God knows what about you. Why don't you go to discos with the girls in your class?"

"For your information," retorted Angel, towering her full inch over her mother, "the bars we go to are a blaze of light. Turns your white shirt blue basking in it. And it's hardly my fault gay men are charged double for the privilege of drinking in a place where they won't get queer-bashed by varmints like my little brother."

"Is that why? Atoning for your brother's sins at the cost of your own liver and dignity?"

"I don't like the girls at school, Mum. And they don't like me."

"Can't say I blame them. Sit there surrounded by all those handsome clean-shaven young men, roaring with laughter when they put balloons inside their frocks and burst each other's bubbles, camping it up in high-pitched voices, and you think you're getting your own back on the girls at school for calling you what you are: a snob, a brat and a show-off."

"Drag shows are an old tradition of gay culture," Angel attempted, "A way of expressing pride in being homosexual in the teeth of oppression."

Shindy was unimpressed. "They're so proud of being gay men they dress up as women to prove it.

129

Your teachers tell me it's become a ritual to throw the fattest girl into the rubbish bin, but you'd hardly justify that on grounds of tradition."

Angel did not answer. She had burst into tears. Shindy looked at her.

"I'm sorry, darling, but I'm not going to treat you like a child when you act like the worst kind of grown up. I'm glad you have gay friends, and I like Gaylord very much, but I do not understand why you're so contemptuous of girls your age and I can only conclude it's some nasty idea those men have put into your head," Shindy paused, "It's not good for a woman to hero-worship men."

"Mum, men are so streamlined, no boobs and bottoms to get in their way. No curse once a month to make them irritable and dirty. And they're generous, not bitchy and penny-pinching like women."

"Well," concluded Shindy, "No fear of you becoming a lesbian."

"How come you know so much about drag shows?" asked Angel a few days later, in a rare departure from youthful self-absorption.

"I think you'll find your grandmother is already only too familiar with the sucking of eggs," said Shindy drily.

"I don't hate him because he's queer," Shindy told her friend Daphnis at work, "I hate him because he's cold and arrogant and because he's my husband. I hate him because he's a snob and bad for the children. Did you know he put Angel down for the Sixth Form at Marlborough, his old school, as soon as he heard they were taking girls? I knew nothing about it till her teacher rang to find out why she'd missed school. Turned out she'd been off sitting the scholarship exam. I mean, can you believe it?"

"Pass the tippex," said Daphnis.

"I only stay because of the children," said Shindy.

"My life's a vista of tippex crusts," said Daphnis.

"Angel is bent on repeating all my mistakes," said Shindy.

"Someone keeps leaving the lids off," said Daphnis, "I wonder if it's me."

"And Hillary seems to have taken up blood sports," said Shindy.

"Course, if I were the perfect typist, I wouldn't need any," said Daphnis.

"Daphnis," said Shindy, "You haven't listened to a word I've said."

"You're not saying anything," said Daphnis.

"I've made an appointment," said Gaylord gloomily.

"Well done," said Angel, "They can cure anything these days."

"I'm not sure I want to be cured," said Gaylord.

"I expect that's part of the treatment," said Angel, "Think how nice it'll be when you're normal."

"Well?" asked Angel, taking the phone into the loo. The cord wouldn't stretch to her bedroom.

"It was awful. So crude, so exactly as one might imagine down to the full colour penises and electric shocks."

"Electric shocks?" repeated Angel.

"They sit you down in front of a big white screen, show you slides of naked, muscle-bound white men, then they give you a light shock. Next come naked white women with wide hips and big breasts. No shock. Simple."

"It's barbaric."

"Oh no," said Gaylord, "Not barbaric. Racist, sexist, brutal and highly sophisticated. Attila the Hun was, after all, not an expert on electricity. At the end of the course I get an NHS prostitute to sleep with."

"Prostitution on the rates?" said Angel.

"They introduce their little show with a preamble about the misery of homosexuality and the evils of buggery."

"I'll be right over."

"Gaylord, something's bitten you. You've got the most frightful bruise on your neck. Oh. But you promised me you wouldn't. Not till you'd tried."

"I tried. If Dr Dun had stuck to telling me how lovely women are, I could only have agreed. But he had to go into great detail about the disgust and disgrace of sodomy and fellatio. As soon as I got out of there I dived into the nearest cottage for a thorough cleansing. Spent the night screwing my ass off, as they say."

"I see," said Angel. "So that's that."

"Why don't you find a nice girl and settle down?" said Gaylord.

"Don't presume to give me advice," stormed Angel, "You sound just like my mother."

With this insult Angel departed. Life seemed to be getting harder.

She had only wanted what was good for Gaylord: to be normal and happy like everyone else. Maybe if he couldn't be normal, she couldn't either. Gaylord thought she should find a girl, did he? Thought he knew what was good for her. But they required so much more, would not settle for as little as men got from each other. Angel did not think she had enough to offer.

As the days went by, Angel felt increasingly that she owed Gaylord an apology. That she had urged him, for reasons more of curiosity and conservatism than anything deep or personal, into doing something any decent human being would despise themselves for. She could not decide whether to write, phone or turn up on his doorstep. If that was what they had in store for gay men, whatever did they do to girls who. . . Angel had not told her mother why it was the girls at school kept away from her. She remembered admiring a classmate's arm, the sun playing along its fine hair, and imagined the electric shock they would administer to make her admire the science master instead. Actually, the rumours and the giggles were as effective as any electric current. In the end she found Gaylord at the tube station telephoning her. She told him she was sorry. He said he was sorry too, and would she like to meet Hunk?

"What are you doing tonight, Shindy?" asked Daphnis.

"Thought I'd cook a romantic little dinner for four, eat mine over the ironing, stick the other three in the oven on a low flame, take last night's out of the oven and leave them to soak, scrub the three from the day before yesterday, dry them and put them away in the dresser," said Shindy.

"Lucky you've got twelve plates," said Daphnis.

"Every so often," said Shindy, "I drop one."

"Why don't you have dinner with me?"

"It's been so long since I ate in front of another human being I've probably forgotten all my table manners."

"As long as you don't start ordering four of everything and warm milk for the baby."

"I'm more likely to tell you to spit on my hanky so I can wipe the side of your mouth," said Shindy.

"I see you've been out on a date before," said Daphnis.

"Alice, this is Hunk. Hunk, meet Alice," said Gaylord with as much enthusiasm as he could muster. Angel was looking distinctly noble. Hunk had spent the last ten minutes assuring Gaylord that he was fond of women, was sure the world would be a different place without them. Gaylord would have preferred to spend the evening in bed with Hunk. Or in the kitchen with Angel, gossiping and giggling and swopping left wing anecdotes, their favourite form of politics. Angel and Hunk surveyed each other.

What does a woman wear to meet her boyfriend's boyfriend? Angel and Shindy had discussed the sartorial proprieties at length. Mrs Beeton, usually such a comfort, had no hint on this, nicest point of etiquette. Shindy had suggested sexual neutrality and clean finger nails, had even lent her daughter her unisex grey trench coat. It was her favourite and Angel was sure to return it grubby and with soggy tissues in both pockets. Still, there was little enough one could do for one's daughter when one was plotting to leave her father. Shindy was relieved Gaylord had found himself a steady boyfriend. So much more natural. Shindy did not really approve of cross sex unions. If God had meant men and women to sleep together He wouldn't have created cervical cancer. Angel was finding sexual neutrality more and more uncomfortable. But the alternative seemed to be accompanied by more volts than she could tolerate.

Hunk had the moustache and yellow V neck sweater of his kind. He had dressed for the bar rather than for Angel and looked as undauntingly familiar as a cherished stereotype or a garden gnome. He smiled benignly down upon the small blonde in the trench coat and, as an afterthought, shook its hand. Better than patting her on the head, thought Gaylord, wincing all the same.

Angel smiled winningly. "Hello, Hunk," she said, "Short for hunker?"

"Hunker?" Hunk repeated blankly as Gaylord raised his eyebrow.

"Squat, bend, cringe," Angel offered.

"Oh no," said Hunk, "It's just a sorta nickname. My mother called me Archy."

"Your father called you Paul. They didn't know what to call you so they called you Archibald," said Angel.

"No, Hunk," said Hunk, looking over her head toward the pool table where a young man was taking off his jacket and rolling up his sleeves. "Melvin and Rodney are here," he announced to Gaylord.

"Shall I hang up your coat?" Gaylord asked Angel.

"I'll keep it on," said Angel.

"It suits you," said Gaylord.

"It suits what, exactly?" enquired Angel.

"It's a very nice colour," said Hunk, "I won't be long."

"Just remember who you came with," called Gaylord.

"And which way up your bread is buttered," muttered Angel.

"As for that," said Gaylord, "It's the other way round."

"Sugar Daddy? That would explain a lot," said Angel, "Wherever did you find him?"

"Page turning in Tonbridge. Turned a page and there he was."

"You mean Hunk's a piano player?"

"Conductor," said Gaylord.

"What was it, then? Fancied the way he twirled his baton?"

"Did I fancy the way he twirled his baton? Alice are you positive, I mean are you absolutely convinced, sure and certain beyond all reasonable doubt, that you have phrased your question exactly as you intended?"

"Yes," said Angel.

"Then I suggest you close Mrs Beeton's chapter on drum majorettes, turn to the index and look up how to behave toward the man your old friend loves."

"You love him?"

Gaylord grinned. "Isn't it wonderful."

"I don't think I've ever loved anyone except my mother and Hillary. And you."

"I loved you too," said Gaylord. "I still do. What's that line? 'We left, as all lovers leave all lovers, much too soon to get the real loving done.'"

"That's terrific," said Angel, "What is it?"

"An American poet, Judy Grahn. She's a dyke. She wrote this really wonderful. . . I keep thinking I'm not the right person to be introducing you to lesbian culture."

"Did I ask you to?" retorted Angel, wondering how you get to meet the right person. Judy Grant, huh. How many volts did they stick into her? But she hadn't let up. A dyke poet, whatever next. Angel smiled to herself, she wanted to jump onto her chair and yell, "Next please".

"You didn't ask me," Gaylord was saying, "But I feel, it's strange, I feel I owe it to you."

"Let me get this straight: you feel, as my gay brother

135

and honourable mentor presumably, that in some strange way you owe me lesbian culture? You feel that lesbian culture is, in some strange way, your possession and so you can offer me a taste of it? You feel. . ."

"I feel that as a man and a twenty-two year old some things are easier for me than for a sixteen year old girl. Hearing about and buying lesbian poetry appears to be one of them. If I didn't think it would be the beginning of losing you, I'd give you a copy of 'A Woman is Talking to Death'."

"Why would you lose me? It's as explosive as that? One poem and you never speak to a man again? Sounds better and better."

"I don't think she intended it that way."

"That too you presume to know, the intentions of this American lesbian."

"Alice, sometimes you're so sharp you'll cut yourself."

"Sounds like you're more afraid I'll cut you."

Gaylord smiled. "You know that line of Grahn's?"

"About leaving too soon for the real loving?"

"Every time I break up with someone I say it to him. Softens the blow. Makes him feel I'm not such a shit after all, so he wasn't such a twit to get involved with me."

"You said it to me," said Angel flatly. "Does that raise me to the level of one of Gaylord's exes? I think we missed out a stage. We never were lovers."

"It makes you the only one I've been honest with. The others, I let them believe I thought it up on the spur of the moment. But it's true nonetheless, every time, as true as the last."

Next time she was home alone Angel took the phone into the toilet, locked the door and rang WH Smith of Streatham High Road.

"Um hello? Hello, er, I'd like to order a book."

"Just a moment, dear, I'll put you through. What kind of book was it?"

"Poetry. It was a poetry book."

"WH Smith, Book Department, can I help you?"

"I'd like to order a book. Please."

"Do you have title, publisher and author's name?"

"It's 'A Woman's Talking to Death' and it's by Judy Grant, or maybe Graham."

"Just checking for you. Sorry, dear. The only title we have by a Judy Graham, is 'Profit in Profiteroles'. That wouldn't be a poetry book, would it?"

"I don't think. . . It, she's, the book is a er lesbian book."

"Oh I see. Well we wouldn't have anything like that here. Not at WH Smith. Not in Streatham. You could try. . ."

"Yes?"

"You might like to try Compendium in Camden Town."

"That's North, isn't it?"

"Yes. How old are you? Bit young for this sort of thing."

"Angel? Angel? Are you in there?" shouted Lemuel, "I don't think it's fair for you to monopolise both the telephone and the loo, do you?"

"That's my father. He wants to use the toilet," said Angel putting the phone down hurriedly.

The shop assistant went back to her order forms. She made a lot of mistakes.

"So what do you think of Hunk?" Gaylord beamed with such joy it would have been churlish to say anything other than 'I'm really happy for you both'. Angel was churlish.

"You married beneath you."

"Between your teeth you say 'beneath'; I sigh and say 'oh lady I would not lie if only I could always lie beneath Hunk'."

"Pity his name's not Keith."

"We queers have to be creative. Why don't you like him?"

"He's stupid."

"He's not stupid. He's sensitive."

"What to? Magnetic North?"

"He's kind, warm, generous. . ."

"And he's good in bed."

"How did you know?"

"I know you."

"Alice, you are going to have to stop being jealous because it is not going to get you anywhere. Ever. Now say something nice about Hunk."

"I like the colour of his sweater."

Angel pulled herself together. Gaylord was her friend. She didn't have any others.

"I think my home is about to run away from me."

"I think it is. What do you expect, sympathy?"

"For starters."

"You refuse to share in my gladness, why should I share your sadness?"

"You sound like a Christian. The Mission did well out of you."

"I am a Christian. A Christian Atheist and so are you. You don't get rid of it merely by disapproving."

"We're going to have a theological discussion? Gaylord, my mother's got a lover."

"So have I. Lot of people do."

"My mother's lover is a woman."

"She wants to double date with me and Hunk?"

"Her lover is plotting to take my mother away."

"I already gave you my speech on jealousy. It applies to women too."

"I just don't understand it. She has a lovely house, an intelligent, hard-working husband, a son and daughter who are crazy about her, and she wants to throw herself away on some filing clerk with bitten finger nails."

"Maybe she bit them."

"Oh you. Think you're such an iconoclast."

"It's you who are setting up the icons, sweetie. 'Devoted Mother', 'Loving wife', 'Proud Homemaker', like coconuts on a shy waiting to be knocked down."

"But you don't expect the coconuts to abdicate."

"If you don't find it disgusting for me to love another man. . ."

"It's different for a woman. And it's even more different if you're someone else's mother. Surely you see that? I mean, you don't have any responsibilities. It doesn't actually matter what you do."

"Thanks."

"You know what I mean. Women are the bedrock of family life, without them there would be social chaos."

"Who would be patient and forebearing and supportive and attentive?"

"Exactly. Sometimes I wonder if my mother really knows what she's doing."

"Well, that answers one thing I've wondered for a long time."

"Which is?"

"With your long blonde hair and your eyes of blue, your diminutive stature and the absence of a 1,000cc motor bike and black leather jacket, I always assumed that you, like me, would be femme. Seems I'm wrong. Your opinion of the true qualities of womanhood will put you, elbow for elbow with the butches."

"'Will'?"

"You're a dyke, Alice. You can live it and love it or hide it and hate it."

"How can I be a dyke when girls don't like me? Maybe I should go interview my mother like Molly Bolt."

"Of course they like you. You just haven't met the right ones. And wherever did you get a copy of 'Rubyfruit Jungle'?"

"WH Smith of Streatham High Road. I gave them the magic words 'Woman is Talking to Death' and 'Judy Grant'."

"Grahn."

"They gave me another two magic words: 'Compendium' and 'Camden Town'. Just like a monopoly board. I asked the man in the shop and he said, sorry, this is politics, women is in the basement. But downstairs there was only a girl serving and I couldn't ask her."

"Oh?"

"What if she were a lesbian?"

"What if?"

"She might have done something."

139

"Fancy yourself don't you."

"She asked me if I was looking for anything in particular."

"You managed not to say 'Yes, your horns'?"

"She said she'd heard Judy Grahn read the poem in the States and it was terribly moving. I said I'd heard Judy Grahn was a lesbian and were there any more like her? She said there was a whole bookcase and she was about to open a whole shop. A whole shop? I said. Well, she said, a feminist bookshop. Is it the same thing? I said. A bookshop has many shelves she said. Do you want something funny, something serious, something romantic or something else? Something else, I said. She sold me a copy of 'Rubyfruit Jungle'."

"I'm impressed," said Gaylord.

"But what am I going to do about my mother?"

"Lend it to her? I'd be more worried about what you're going to do about you."

"Why don't you leave him?" asked Daphnis.

"It's not him," said Shindy. "It's them."

"I thought you weren't too keen on them," said Daphnis.

"I love them," protested Shindy hotly. "I just don't like their attitude. I must have brought them up all wrong. Maybe they'd be better off without me."

There were things Daphnis didn't understand. How vulnerable the children were. How much it grieved Shindy to see her daughter take after Lemuel. Angel asking for help with her modern history: the role of the USA in the ending of the Second World War. Lemuel's careful, detailed, excruciating explanation. Long past boredom, way past irritation, Angel sat motionless, her face closed, waiting for it to be over. Next time she would ask her mother, who would say, in a vague, world-weary way, "Oh, they won it, the war, the Americans. Everyone, everyone else lost." Only it didn't end, her father's voice did not stop. If Angel had been noisily scribbling notes: "Wait, wait, say that again, you're going too fast"; "How do you spell 'Armistice', Daddy?"; "But what were the

Russians doing?", perhaps her father would have wound down, remembered his role. Lemuel began, instead, to answer the question which had not been asked: "What did you do in the war, Daddy?". "I was a torturer, darling. But it's alright, I only tortured Germans."

Lemuel had been a War Major, in Intelligence because of his near-native German, a language which Shindy had banned from her house. He told his family all about his war work in careful, excruciating detail. Shindy, unable to unlearn her husband's exploits, endeavoured to save her children's ears.

"I don't think Angel needs to know that, Lemuel," she said.

"I think she does," said Lemuel, "I think she does."

Does the Army not provide an after care service for the confessions of its officers? At his prep school, when he was eight years old, Lemuel had been summoned to the headmaster's study for throwing another boy downstairs. Asked why, he replied, "Because otherwise he would have thrown me down." Was that the kind of education he wanted for his daughter?

Lemuel continued his seamless store of anecdotes, secrets wrested, confidences despoiled.

"Most of them were only too happy to talk. Glad to be of interest. Of course one had more respect for the few who kept silent, who tried to keep silent. But it was war. . ."

"Red lips are not so red.
As the stained stones
Kissed by our English dead," quoted Shindy, suddenly, fiercely. At first simply because the poem came to mind, then because it blocked Lemuel out. She continued with the Irish airman who neither loved nor hated but died all the same.

"Do not go gentle into that good night," Shindy rolled and thundered against the dying of the light.

"In Flanders Plain in Northern France,

They're all doing a brand new dance," she started
up brightly. By now Hillary had joined her.

"Getting dizzy and out of breath,
And it's called the dance of death."

Lemuel fixed his beautiful tired eyes on Angel and
began to explain when it is that even officers crack.
Angel, sitting on the floor, looked down at her
homework, at her inky fingers, at her mother and her
little brother side by side on the sofa shrieking out the
death poetry of romantic men, at her father in the
armchair, the light behind him, confessing intricate
cruelty committed in the name of glory and the
children of Britain. There were sides, you had to take
sides, not even homework was safe.

"An Austrian Army awfully arrayed," Shindy began
indomitably. It had been a favourite of Angel's when
she was little.

"Boldly by battery besieged Belgrade," chanted
Hillary, laughing at the change of tone.

"Cossack commanders cannonading come," Angel
capitulated to the voices of protested innocence.

"Deal devastation, dire destructive doom," the three
of them finished the round.

Lemuel got to his feet, still gazing at his daughter,
put on his navy blue great coat and went out the front
door. A few hours later he returned, joined Hillary on
the sofa to watch "The Birdman of Alcatraz". Shindy
brought him a cup of tea.

Shindy felt ashamed. Felt, increasingly as the evening
wore on, that she had not set her children a good
example. Angel should not be taught to counter men
with nonsense rhymes. It was no protection. Shindy
lay on the bed she shared with the children's father
and thought about Daphnis. She thought about her
ankles and her shoulders, the way she walked,
sleeveless and barefoot on the office carpet. Who
would know, watching her on the tube in the
mornings, a neat figure in a neat grey suit, that she
would take off her jacket, take off her shoes, and glide
like butter on Shindy's bread. This time, however hard

Shindy tried, the whole of Daphnis would not come. She was left with the soft skin of her lover's high-arched foot, the brown mutiny of her lover's sulking shoulder. Lemuel came into the bedroom, stared at Shindy lying luxuriant on the bed, seemed about to shout, or stammer, then left carrying the cord of his dressing gown like a clutched straw.

"Daphnis?" whispered Shindy into the telephone, "I'm leaving him. I can't stay just to protect Angel. I don't owe her my life."

Angel made up her mind.

"Good evening," she said to the cab driver, fear making her formal, "Please take me to the club where the women go."

"Hop in," said the cabbie.

Angel gazed at the sign, "Members Only", but was not to be put off. She stood back as a gang of women went down the steps and, recognising a white rabbit when she saw one, followed after.

"She with you?" called the woman on the door.

One of the gang looked up at Angel.

"Sure she is. Come on, Angel. Buy you a drink."

"What you want?"

"Orange juice," said Angel.

"That's okay, Angel. I'll get you a beer or something. Glass of white wine?"

"I'm sick of beer and white wine and shandy and dry sherry and Baby Cham and sweet martini and gin and whiskey and Tia Maria and Bloody Mary. I want a glass of orange juice."

"I'll see if they have any."

The woman came back. "You're in luck, Angel. The nice barmaid is prepared to feed you neat orange juice."

Angel smiled.

"So what do I call you? If I keep on with Angel you'll think we never met."

143

"My gay friends call me Alice."

"Because of your propensity for bolting down rabbit holes?"

Angel smiled again.

"Well, I'm going to stick to Angel. I think it suits you."

"I think it does," said Angel.

"Okay, Angel. I'm SugarBeth. See you around."

SugarBeth bowed preposterously and rejoined her friends.

That wasn't meant to happen. Angel sat back and stared around the room. It was so much smaller, darker and dirtier than the men's bars. Angel glanced across to SugarBeth's table. When the gay boys bought each other drinks they stayed the night. What had she done wrong? SugarBeth was already deep in conversation with one of her buddies. She'd got Angel into the club, bought her a drink, introduced herself, what more did Angel want? Angel gazed at her. SugarBeth was enormously fat and enormously beautiful. She had short dark hair which curled across her cheek bones and dark brown eyes you could drown in. Angel would have drowned had not SugarBeth looked away. Angel tried to ration herself to two glances per minute, but it wasn't enough, so she decided it didn't count if she only gazed at SugarBeth's hands. Then she blushed: SugarBeth would think she was staring at her fat. Now Angel didn't know where to look. How could she get SugarBeth to talk without sounding like she only wanted to go to bed? Maybe she did just want to go to bed. It is amazing how swiftly the transition can be made between sexually latent and sexually potent. It is amazing. But it did not amaze Angel. She was busy.

Angel raised her eyes from the pool of beer on the table in time to catch SugarBeth's wink as she crossed the floor to the loo. Angel had spent the last two years watching men arrange their sex lives; it had left her no useful lessons. The women in the bar reminded her more of the girls at school, with their best friends and sensible shoes, than the glittering gay boys. Angel followed SugarBeth to the loo.

"Thanks for getting me in here," said Angel.

"Oh it's you again," said SugarBeth. "The joke's maybe wearing thin, but you did look like a little white rabbit up there on the stair."

"I felt like one," said Angel, sophistication slipping.

"First time?" asked SugarBeth.

What could Angel say but yes?

Angel stroked SugarBeth's hand, across the back of the knuckles, up the blade of each finger, then into the soft skin in between. She turned it over, swirled her finger tip in the palm of SugarBeth's hand.

"Your body fills me with luxury," she said.

When she looked into SugarBeth's eyes the shock jolted through her. Was this what the men in white coats had been trying to simulate? Angel could not look away this time. Her pants were drenched. SugarBeth's mouth was so soft and moist and red and had no connection with the stained stones of our English dead.

"Will you come home with me?" asked SugarBeth softly.

Angel nodded. "I'll have to ring my mother. Oh God, she'll be furious. Alright for her, but not for me."

"How do you mean?" frowned SugarBeth.

"I'd like to tell you," said Angel, "At great length. If you want to listen."

"I'll listen to anything with you full length," said SugarBeth. Angel winced.

"I'm sorry," said SugarBeth. "I want to know. I want to know you. I want a lot of things."

"My mother has a lesbian," Angel announced. "I mean a lover. My mother is a lesbian. Doesn't it sound weird?"

"Your mother's daughter is a lesbian," said Sugar-Beth.

"Yes," said Angel. "But my mother will not be delighted. She'll think it's all her fault."

"Why don't you telephone her lover?" suggested SugarBeth. "Ask her to explain."

145

"Hello, Daphnis? This is Angel Travers. Have I woken you? I'm sorry."

"What's wrong? You alright? What's happened?"

"I've fallen in love, Daphnis," said Angel proudly, "And I want you to let my mother know I won't be home tonight. I'm going to sleep with SugarBeth Boyd."

The pomposity of sixteen year olds would never cease to amaze Daphnis. Careful not to wake Shindy, Daphnis replied, "Congratulations, darling," and, for the second time that night, "You took your time about it."

MORE RADICAL FEMINIST LESBIAN BOOKS
from ONLYWOMEN PRESS

FICTION

STRANGER THAN FISH: short stories
J.E. Hardy
Rich details of place and fully realised characters narrating: the turbulence of "coming out", the world weary knowledge of relationships with heretofore hetero-sexuals, the damage as well as the enduring love found within family ties.
£4.95   ISBN 0–906500–32–X

A NOISE FROM THE WOODSHED: short stories
Mary Dorcey
Specifically sensual, altogether humorous, feminist lan-guage presenting: escape from an "old age asylum"; expatriate Irish lesbians confronting English racism; heterosexual rural Ireland; "romance" in a variety of guises. *One of the "top twenty" in Feminist Book Fortnight '90.*
£4.95   ISBN 0–906500–30–3

IN AND OUT OF TIME: lesbian feminist fiction anthology
ed. by Patricia Duncker
Eighteen new stories with variety and experiment as the collection's hallmark. The settings — glaciers in Antarctica, the bar of a posh Dublin hotel, the Mediterranean in the time of Sappho, suburban white country clubs, London tube trains, gay bars in South Africa of the 60s, interracial discos in today's England — frame issues of racism, sex and disability, booze, romance and independence.
£4.95   ISBN 0–906500–37–0

BULLDOZER RISING
Anna Livia
Futuristic novel of bone chilling glee. In a hi-tech city where good citizens must die at 41, a secret congress of "old" women love, quarrel, plot survival and fight back.
£4.95   ISBN 0–906–500–27–3

RELATIVELY NORMA
Anna Livia
Anna Livia's first novel — about a London feminist coming out to her family in Australia
£3.95   ISBN 0—906500—10—9

INCIDENTS INVOLVING WARMTH: lesbian feminist love stories
Anna Livia
A collection which interprets love with bittersweet humour and wryly accurate observations — "dangerous dykes", devious grandmothers and very perceptive eleven year olds.
£3.95   ISBN 0—906500—21—4

ALTOGETHER ELSEWHERE
Anna Wilson
A novel about women as vigilantes: wage clerks, laundrette workers, mothers — black and white, lesbian and straight. Fiction which demands reflection.
"its language is taut and precise ... makes the pulse race."
City Limits

£3.95   ISBN 0—906500—18—4

CACTUS
Anna Wilson
Realism in Anna Wilson's lyrically graceful first novel about lesbians within the social pressures of contemporary England and those of twenty years ago.
£3.95   ISBN 0—906500—04—4

SATURDAY NIGHT IN THE PRIME OF LIFE
Dodici Azpadu
Tough, tightly written novel about lesbianism in the long term — as one of the characters says, "Queer begins at sixty."
£3.95   ISBN 0—906500—24—9

GOAT SONG
Dodici Azpadu
Urban, dyke street-life in a novel which looks at the excitement, the danger and, ultimately, the profound

moral dignity of its characters.
£3.95   ISBN 0—906500—25—7

THE NEEDLE ON FULL: science fiction short stories
Caroline Forbes
More than dykes-in-space; stories that show us a range of
all-too-probable futures, stories that crackle with wit and
urgency.
£4.95   ISBN 0—906500—19—2

THE PIED PIPER: lesbian feminist fiction anthology (1989)
ed. by Anna Livia and Lilian Mohin
Work by 19 authors with landscapes that change as you
move from one story to the next: medieval Britain, 19th
century Jamaica, modern southern France, dyke bars in
the U.S.A. and London. Between them they touch on
many myths and issues: "passing", definitions of activism,
definitions of love.
£4.95   ISBN 0—906500—29—X

THE REACH: lesbian feminist fiction anthology
ed. by Lilian Mohin and Sheila Shulman
The first in Britain and still being reprinted for its gripping
writing, its wide range of subjects: family confrontations
and connections, futuristic fantasies, struggles with anti-
lesbianism, the exhilaration of love.
£3.95   ISBN 0—906500—15—X

THEORY

FOR LESBIANS ONLY: a Separatist Anthology
ed. by Sarah Lucia Hoagland & Julia Penelope
The world's first anthology of lesbian separatism. 608
pages documenting twenty years of both activism and
scholarship. Novelists, poets, musicians, philosophers and
rowdy dykes contribute here to a declaration of lesbian
civilisation.
"something to cut through the late 1980s 'post-feminist'
confusion like a hot knife through butter"
The Pink Paper

£8.95   ISBN 0—906500—28—1

LOVE YOUR ENEMY?
heterosexual feminism and political lesbianism
The debate as originally seen in letters to "WIRES".
"essential reading for anyone trying to work out how
feminists view lesbianism"   *Undercurrents*
£2.95   ISBN 0–906500–08–7

WOMEN AGAINST VIOLENCE AGAINST WOMEN
ed. by Sandra McNeill & dusty rhodes
Three sets of conference papers discussing pornography,
rape and feminist action.
£4.95   ISBN 0–906500–16–8

BREACHING THE PEACE
Collection of essays from a Radical Feminist conference
anti the women's peace movement.
£1.25   ISBN 0–906500–13–3

DOWN THERE
Sophie Laws
An illustrated guide to self-exam.
£1.50   ISBN 0–906500–05–2

WOMEN AND HONOR
Adrienne Rich
Prose from one of Lesbian Feminism's foremost poets.
"to extend the possibilities of truth between us. The
possibility of life between us."
£0.75 (pamphlet)   ISBN 0–906500–02–8

POETRY

BECAUSE OF INDIA: selected poems and fables
Suniti Namjoshi
Work spanning 9 published books and accompanied by
essays which situate these deft, precise poems in the time,
place and sexual politics which surrounded their writing. A
landmark publication. *One of the "top twenty" in Feminist
Book Fortnight '90.*
"blending that which is uncompromisingly Indian in her
with the best of the English satirical tradition ... demon-

strates how effectively the personal may be fused with the
political." *SpareRib*
£4.95   ISBN 0—906500—33—8

PASSION IS EVERYWHERE APPROPRIATE
Caroline Griffin
Memorably rhythmic verse in the first full collection from a
much anthologised poet. Poems that wring an exhilarating
energy from the ordinary detail of contemporary British
lesbian life.
"the journey towards oneself requires courage and
honesty. Both qualities are here ... always earthed in the
experience of feminist lesbianism" *City Limits*
£3.95   ISBN 0—906500—34—6

LOVE, DEATH and the CHANGING of the SEASONS
Marilyn Hacker
A novel in verse. Sonnets recounting the heady start
through to the rending conclusion of a one-year love affair.
"virtuoso displays of poetic craftsmanship"
Poetry Review

£4.95   ISBN 0—906500—26—5

BEAUTIFUL BARBARIANS: lesbian feminist poetry
ed. by Lilian Mohin
An anthology that concentrates, rather than collects;
displaying the work of sixteen poets (with photos and
biographical notes).
"juicy and contentious" *Everywoman*
£4.95   ISBN 0—906500—23—0

ONE FOOT ON THE MOUNTAIN: British Feminist Poetry
1969—1979
ed. by Lilian Mohin
Not just the first — still the one that changes lives.
£4.95   ISBN 0—906500—01—X

DIFFERENT ENCLOSURES
Irena Klepfisz
Work from three collections by a major Jewish lesbian
feminist poet.
£3.95   ISBN 0—906500—17—6

THE WORK OF A COMMON WOMAN
Judy Grahn
A poetry of love and activism, the heart of the women's
liberation movement.
£3.95   ISBN 0—906500—20—6

Free catalogue from:
Onlywomen Press, 38 Mount Pleasant, London
WC1X 0AP

*If ordering books, please include 15% for packing and
postage. Prices may change from those listed here. We
endeavour to keep them as low as possible.*